Whisper of Lightning

Jessica Hemingway

ISBN 978-0-473-27228-9

Cover by Julie Duffy

Table of Contents

Chapter One

"Good bones."

Hearing his comment, heat rose to Jaz Sinclair's face as she tucked a lock of hair behind her ears and thanked her gene pool for her high cheekbones and aquiline nose. In vain she tried to remember the builder's name.

"But there's a damp patch in the master bedroom," he continued, scribbling notes on his clipboard. "Easily fixed by replacing the rotten window frame."

With a stab of disappointment she realised his bone comment pertained to the old house and not to her physical attributes.

He strode across the dining room and prodded the corners of the wooden window frame, nodding his head. "This one's fine. Basically the house needs some plastering, the gutters need attention, and some of the roof tiles need replacing. Other than that, this old place is in pretty good nick."

Through the dirty window pane she glanced at his van parked on the circular gravel driveway. His name was emblazoned in dark blue paint on the side of the white vehicle: Rick Moron. She did a double take. Whoops! Not Moron, Moran, Rick Moran. She must get her eyes checked.

Jaz followed him as he wandered out of the room, down the black and white tiled hallway and into the library. Oak bookshelves filled with leather bound volumes lined the walls, and a large desk, its surface scarred from decades of use, stood on a threadbare Turkish carpet. A cracked leather sofa, with deep seats was littered with brightly coloured cushions. Resting its head on its front paws a large grey cat splayed along the back of the sofa, scowling at the intrusion. It swished its tail and watched. Rick stood in the centre of the room, turning slowly in a circle, his eyes roaming the walls and ceiling.

"It's an amazing room, isn't it?" she said. Pools of colour illuminated the room as afternoon sunshine filtered through the lead lights. She stroked the cat's head; he raised his chin and purred. "I've always loved it. It's the ideal place to curl up with a good book."

"There's something wrong with it," Rick said. "The proportions are wrong."

Jaz couldn't see anything wrong; to her eyes the room was perfect.

Rick placed the clipboard on the desk. From the back pocket of his jeans he took a metal measuring tape, handed her the end and pointed to the outside wall. Obediently, she held it under the windowsill while he stretched the tape to the opposite wall and checked the measurement. The cat jumped to the ground, threading itself in and out of her legs, then accompanied them as they left the room.

In the hallway Jaz helped Rick take another measurement, and then followed him into the dining room where he checked its length. He scratched his head, muttering to himself as he pressed the button and the metal tape rattled back into its housing. The startled cat dashed up the stairs, stopping close to the top and peering down at them through the barley twist banister rails. Rick's work boots clumped on the tiled floor as he returned to the library. She followed, wondering what was bothering him, and hoping it wouldn't be expensive to fix.

"This room has definitely been altered, there's over a metre and half missing. It's well done though, the coving is excellent, but they should have moved the ceiling rose. Dead giveaway that," he said, pointing at the light fitting. He removed several heavy volumes from a mid-level shelf. Dust motes rose and he sneezed. "Do you know when the alterations were done?"

"No. It's always been like this."

"How long have you lived here?"

"I've not lived here for almost a decade, but the house has belonged to my family for over eighty years, so I've been coming here all my life. I inherited it a couple of months ago." Grief squeezed her heart, and she held onto the edge of the desk to steady herself, not wanting to display any sign of sadness in front of this stranger.

"Are you going to keep it?" He added another stack of books to the pile on the desk.

She ran her hand over the embossed cover of the top volume. "No. I can't afford to live here. I thought I'd do a bit of renovating, possibly get a new bathroom, and then put it on the market."

Rick cleared the last of the books off the shelf, and leant into the space. He knocked on the plaster wall with his knuckles. "It's rock solid, not a flimsy partition. It's been bricked up for some reason."

Jaz shivered as her imagination moved into overdrive and she remembered an old movie she'd seen where a man had been bricked up alive and left to die of starvation. Could there be a skeleton behind the wall? She hugged herself as she peered at the smooth plaster. "Why would it have been bricked up?"

He shrugged. "Your guess is as good as mine."

"What should I do about it?"

"Whatever you want. You can leave it as it is if you like. Given you're planning to sell, that would be the cheapest option." He began replacing the books on the shelf.

Jaz checked her watch. "Sorry, I need to go. I've an appointment in Coppington and I don't want to be late. Leave the books, I'll do them later."

Picking up her handbag, she showed him out. The small stones of the gravel driveway crunched beneath their feet as they walked towards their cars.

Unlocking his van, he said, "I'll drop the quote off soon."

He tossed the clipboard onto the dashboard and swung into the driver's seat.

"Great. The sooner the work starts the better."

She took a screwdriver from her bag and headed towards her car. The old orange Mini had seen better days. Some months ago, the key had broken off in the lock; she'd managed to extricate it with a pair of pliers, but still hadn't had a new one cut. She figured nobody in his right mind would steal her car, so didn't bother locking it. She slid into the driver's seat and inserted the screwdriver under the dash, twisted it a couple of times and waited for the engine to fire up.

The country roads to Coppington took a little longer than the dual carriageway, but Jaz preferred sacrificing the additional minutes in order to enjoy the tranquil pastoral scenes before dealing with the bustling town and its one-way system from hell. Even waiting at road works for the youth holding the stop sign to turn it to go didn't faze her as she watched black-faced lambs gambolling in a field.

Joining the frenzied traffic in Coppington she scanned the streets looking for a parking space. After driving around the town centre twice, and losing a spot to a hulking great Range Rover she finally managed to squeeze the Mini into a tiny spot. She hurried around the corner and into the modern interior of Harrington's art gallery, cursing herself for being late. Not the good first impression she'd hoped to make.

On the opposite side of the room, Jaz spotted a woman examining a small abstract painting. A chic black cashmere dress skimmed the woman's skeletally thin body. Her thick ebony hair, cut in the latest style, swung around her shoulders as she turned towards the door, revealing her pale face split by a gash of dramatically arresting plum lipstick. She was every bit as exquisite as any of the exhibited art works. Jaz straightened her skirt and checked that her blouse buttons hadn't gaped across her bust. Despite being dressed in her smartest outfit, the woman's sleek perfection left Jaz feeling dowdy and dishevelled. She tried to smooth her rampant wavy hair without success.

"You must be Jasmine; you look just like your mother!" The woman walked towards her, hand outstretched; her nail polish the same colour as her smiling lips. "I'm Annabel Harrington."

Jaz shook her hand, hardly able to believe that her mother had chosen this woman as her agent. Annabel looked so worldly and smart whereas her mother didn't — strike that — her mother hadn't given two hoots about her appearance and slopped around in baggy track pants or ancient kaftans. Jaz relaxed a little as she realised Annabel mustn't judge people by their appearance. "Hello. Sorry if I'm a little late. Parking's a nightmare."

Annabel grimaced. "Yes, I should have thought to warn you. It's market day. Now, come through to the office where we can talk."

In complete contrast to the pristine gallery and the sleekness of Annabel's appearance, the office was mired in a chaotic swamp of paper. Posters, flyers and postcards for a variety of upcoming and past exhibitions spilled from their boxes, covering the desk, shelves and most of the floor space. Careful not to pierce anything with her heels, Jaz picked her way through the assorted mounds to a chair.

"I know this must be a difficult time for you, but we do have to finalise a few details for your mother's show. I've got a mock up of the exhibition catalogue here for you," said Annabel, delving into a foot high pile of papers and tugging out a glossy booklet. "Do you approve?"

Jaz took the booklet. Her finger traced the detail from a familiar painting. A blaze of rich colour bled across the cover and encircled the artist's name: Theresa Sinclair. Her mother. Jaz bit her lip, and flicked through the pages, stopping briefly at the black and white photograph of her mother painting in her studio. Her vision blurred. She blinked back the tears and willed herself to stay in control. She wouldn't fall to pieces in front of Annabel.

Jaz closed the catalogue, held it on her lap. "It looks good. The colours have come out well. Mum would be delighted, I'm sure."

"I plan to use a close-up of one of the glass bottles on the posters. She used them in so many of her paintings. Do you know why?"

"No, she never told me." Since her mother's death she'd become aware of how much she didn't know about her. When she came home she'd thought they'd have plenty of time together, but her mother had been snatched away after a few short weeks. "The bottles are part of my great-grandmother's collection. They're all extremely old; ancient would be a more accurate description. Some are well over a thousand years old."

"They should be in a museum."

Jaz nodded. "The old house is like a museum. My great-grandfather was an archaeologist so there are lots of interesting artefacts to inspire an artist. Mum used quite a lot of them over the years."

Impressed by the clarity and quality of the prints, Jaz thumbed through the catalogue again. "Did you have a particular picture in mind for the poster?"

"Yes. I love the one with the hands."

Jaz found the image. "I know the story behind this one. It's part of my family history."

Annabel's eyes widened and she clasped her hands. "Do tell."

"Nannalu — that's what we called my great-grandmother Lucinda — was a bit of a blue stocking and worked at the British Museum when she graduated. She was travelling in Turkey with a group of friends when she spotted the bottle tucked away at the back of a stall in a bazaar. She was so captivated by the bottle she didn't notice a man also making a beeline for it. As they both reached towards it his hand brushed against hers sending a jolt of electricity shooting up her arm."

Annabel shifted to the front of her seat, her face eager. "But Lucinda got it?"

Jazz laughed. "I'm afraid not. The man, however, acted chivalrously and let her barter for it. She haggled for all she was worth but, despite her best efforts, couldn't meet the trader's price, and so she left disappointed."

Annabel slumped back. "Oh, what a pity. So this picture is Theresa's interpretation of that moment."

"Yes. But the story gets better. Nannalu wasn't alone in feeling the jolt of passion when their hands made contact. A few hours later the man with the electric fingers turned up at her hotel, and offered her the bottle in exchange for having dinner with him. She was overwhelmed that the stranger would be prepared to give her such a precious gift. Long story short — she agreed to go to dinner and they fell in love. He was my great-grandfather. So in the end they both had the bottle. It's funny, if it hadn't been for that bottle I might not have existed."

"How fabulous." Annabel scribbled a note on a post-it and added it to the collection around her computer screen. "Perhaps we could have the bottle on show at the exhibition. Would you mind?"

Awkward to be handling the minutiae of the exhibition, Jaz wished her mother had made all of the decisions. She pondered Annabel's suggestion for a moment, wondering what her mother would do. What if she got it wrong? But what could be wrong about exhibiting a bottle? Nothing as far as she was concerned. She made her decision. "I don't see why not, as long as it's in a cabinet or something. Mind you, I'm not sure where it is. Now you've brought it up, I can't remember seeing it in the house since I came back. All the others are on Nanalu's display stand."

"Well, if it turns up... I'd also be keen to display any sketchbooks that pertain to this series of paintings."

"I'll have a look in Mum's studio, see what's there." A lump of raw emotion rose in Jaz's throat. She gulped it away and fiddled with the bangles that adorned her wrist. "I've not been in there since she died."

"It must be hard for you." Annabel reached across the desk and patted Jaz's arm, gave her a minute to compose herself before continuing briskly. "But, didn't you prepare the canvases for the photographer?"

"No. I gave her the key and left her to it. She gave me the impression she knew what she was doing."

"She's more than competent and a bit of a perfectionist; she's been doing the photos of your mother's work for the last five years. Now, we need to arrange collection of the canvases." Annabel tapped some keys on her keyboard and checked the diary. "What about two weeks on Monday?"

"That should be fine." Jaz rummaged in her bag, couldn't find a pen, so borrowed one from Annabel and jotted the date on the back of her hand. She'd transfer it to the calendar when she returned home.

"So have you thought what you will do with the money?"

"I'm doing some renovations on the house before I sell it, so I'll put it towards that."

Annabel's eyes opened wide "You're selling the house?"

"I can't afford to keep it." A wave of sadness washed over her as she contemplated selling her family home. "I wish I could."

Annabel leaned back in her chair and stretched her legs out, upsetting a pile of postcards and fanning them across the floor. She ignored them. "Jaz, do you realise how much your mother's paintings are worth?"

"Not really. We never discussed it. I know she got by."

"Got by!" Annabel laughed. "Jaz, Theresa Sinclair is one of the hottest names in the art world. Collectors are desperate to get their hands on her work."

Jaz sucked in her breath. "Really?"

"Really. Since her exhibition at the Liverpool Tate two years ago, she hasn't been able to produce work fast enough to meet demand. And, I hate to say it, but now she's no longer with us her prices have gone through the roof. Don't throw anything away! Even the tiniest sketch will be hotly fought over. You'll not need to worry about money for quite a while."

"Wow. She's really that famous? I...I'd no idea."

Annabel held out her hands, palms upwards, in a gesture of disbelief. "How come you don't know?"

Jaz chewed on her lip and thought for a second. "Well, she was just Mum to me. I always loved her paintings, but I didn't realise everybody else did too. I've been living overseas. I'd only been back about six weeks when the accident happened."

Annabel picked her way to a filing cabinet and rifled through a drawer. She pulled out a folder, leafed through the contents and removed several sheets of paper. "Here, you can take these. They're copies of newspaper and magazine articles about her work. There's quite a bit online too if you do a search."

Jaz flicked through the pile of paper Annabel handed her. "I can't believe she never showed me these. If they were my reviews I'd be shouting from the rooftops."

"she could hardly believe it herself. She wasn't comfortable in the limelight."

"That's true. She hated being the centre of attention, always happier in the background, watching the action. All the same, I'd have loved to shared her success."

"It's a shame you'll have to do it retrospectively, but at least you can honour her memory. Money's going to be the least of your worries from now. Theresa had a stack of old canvases that she'd either not sold or not exhibited. She showed them to me when I visited her studio. They were stored in one of the outhouses. We can release one or two onto the market every now and then. A slow trickle will be much more lucrative than flooding the market."

"I don't know what to say." Jaz struggled to find words to convey her relief at being able to keep her family home, and the shock of her mother's formidable reputation. Her mother had always been modest about her talent, and Jaz, who knew little about art appreciation, had been too wrapped up in her own life to realise that her mother's career had bloomed.

Chapter Two

The cat padded into the hallway and miaowed a greeting when Jaz returned. She loved the way he always did that, it made the house feel occupied, made her feel needed.

"Hiya, Whisper." She bent to ruffle the fur under his chin. "Good news. We don't have to move house." She picked him up and did a little dance. He wriggled from her arms and hopped back to the ground.

"How do you fancy a nice tin of tuna to celebrate?" In the kitchen, Jaz opened the pantry door and scoured the shelves for the can of fish. Her eyes alighted on a bunch of keys hanging from a hook screwed into the edge of a shelf. The keys for the outhouses. She picked them up, weighed them in her hand and went to the window. She looked out at the garden, tracing the path. The lush lawns, surrounded by herbaceous borders, led to an abundant rose garden, already resplendent with scented blooms. Beyond the rose garden the path split, one branch going to the vegetable garden and the other to the creeper-clad stone wall of her mother's studio and the other outbuildings. A chill crept across her shoulders, and she tried to rub some warmth into them. She should check in there for the missing bottle, and she'd promised Annabel to locate some sketchbooks for the exhibition, but she wasn't ready.

Her stomach churned, her throat constricted.

Maybe she'd have a look tomorrow. There was no rush after all. Jaz dropped the keys onto the worktop and clicked the switch on the kettle. As she dropped a teabag into a chipped china mug, she realised she couldn't keep avoiding the studio. The thought of it had hovered over her for weeks, the longer she put it off the bigger and more difficult the task became. Burying her mother had been the hardest thing she'd ever had to do, and yet somehow she'd survived that ordeal. In comparison, entering the studio should be a piece of cake. Her reticence puzzled her. Logic told her there was nothing to fear, but her guts said otherwise.

The clatter of the cat flap captured her attention. Tail held aloft, Whisper pranced across the grass. He stopped under the cascading yellow blossoms of a laburnum tree, looked towards the studio, then cocked his head and stared at her.

"I'm not ready," she mouthed at him.

Steam from the kettle misted the windowpane and obliterated her view. Threads of burnt sienna coloured tea seeped from the teabag as she drowned it in boiling water. The colour intensified, swirling and dissipating, jogging a memory of a paintbrush being cleaned in a jam jar of water.

Aching emptiness enveloped her. Weighed down by a bottomless sadness she had a sudden longing to be close to her mother, and if she could no longer be close to her then at least to be close to her things, to the place her mother had been happiest.

Jaz grabbed the keys, hugged them to her chest and resolved to conquer her fear. After that, everything else would be easy. She opened the back door and stepped onto the lawn.

When she drew level with Whisper he came to his feet and fell into step beside her. His easy feline gait contrasted with the stiffness of her tense posture. She took a deep breath and rolled her shoulders trying to loosen up.

The sun's rays bounced off the grey stone outbuildings looming in front of her. A tracery of Virginia creeper climbed up the gable end to the rooftop. Paint had peeled from the doors and window frames exposing bare wood. Pansies, petunias and trailing lobelia spilled from an old stone trough now employed as a planter. In its picturesque quaintness the scene could easily have been the subject of a painting.

Jaz focused on the studio door, and finally understood the anxiety roiling in her stomach. Grief. Consumed by loss, tears welled and blurred her vision as she fumbled with the keys and tried to unlock the door. On the third attempt the tumblers turned. She took a deep breath and pushed the door open. The hinges squealed and the bottom of the door scratched at the concrete floor, then all was quiet.

She stood on the doorstep, her hand pressed on the jamb. Whisper slipped into the room and jumped onto a rickety wooden chair. He curled up on the fat cushion and closed his eyes, obviously at home in the studio.

Flecks of dust glistened and danced in the sunlight streaming through the windows and skylights. The walls sported a selection of paintings in various stages of completion. Her mother had always worked on several pieces at a time. A delicate film of cobwebs floated and stretched from a bare light bulb to a half finished canvas propped on an easel.

The familiar smells of linseed oil and turpentine evoked powerful memories of her mother working. Fear dissipated as peace settled on Jaz's soul and she entered her mother's world. She batted away the cobweb, glad its maker was nowhere to be seen as she flicked the sticky residue from her fingers. She wandered around the studio caressing paintbrushes and touching twisted tubes of paint with exotic names: phthalo green, quinacridone crimson, purple madder, cerulean blue.

Finished canvases stacked on end filled the spaces of a rough vertical storage system. One at a time, she drew them out, recognising them from the photographs in the exhibition catalogue Annabel had shown her. The colourful compositions were more striking in real life. However good the photographs, they failed to capture the dexterity of the brush strokes, the lightness of her mother's touch, the luminous quality of the paint.

She wanted to touch the painting. Her hand hovered for a few seconds before she snatched it away. Her mother wouldn't approve. She knew her mother often applied the paint with her fingers pushing the colours into each other. She wanted to touch what her mother had touched. Unable to resist she ran her fingers over the surface of the magnificent painting of the bottle and hands, feeling the slight give of the canvas, the texture of the paint.

She removed the half finished canvas from the easel and leant it against the wall, and then put the hands painting in its place. The intense colours of the bottle reached out to her. She stepped back to better view it. Her heart lifted. Perhaps she'd keep this painting for herself, not let some stranger have the joy of ownership.

She tried to remember whether the bottle truly looked so splendid, or had artistic licence helped. She hadn't seen it in over five years.

"Where did she put it?" she asked Whisper.

He lifted an eyelid, looked at her briefly, before letting it drop again.

Jaz scoured the shelves and cupboards under the workbench. No bottle. She tried the drawers on a battered metal filing cabinet, but they refused to give. Excitement bubbled inside her. Of course her mother would have locked the bottle away; surely anything that old must be valuable. She located the lock and tried the small keys on the bunch. One of them worked and she slid the top drawer open. No bottle, but she had located her mother's sketchbooks.

The other drawers yielded more sketchbooks, but still no bottle.

Jaz sat on the paint spattered concrete floor and began looking through the books.

"Jasmine! Is that you in there?"

The gravelly sound of a man's voice startled her. She recognised it immediately. Only one person called her Jasmine now her mother had gone. She jumped to her feet.

Ted's frame filled the doorway. He wore a misshapen T-shirt and a pair of drooping brown trousers. His weather beaten face crinkled as he smiled at her. "Ah, it is you."

"Hi, Ted." She went to the door and they stepped into the garden.

Ted had been doing the gardening and odd jobs at the house for as long as Jaz could remember. She'd spent a lot of time trailing him in her childhood and he'd been the only long-term male influence in her life.

"Come to look at your mum's stuff have you?"

"I'm looking for her recent sketchbooks for her exhibition."

"If they're not in there, have a look in the shed next door. There are a lot of old paintings and stuff in there." He pointed at his wheelbarrow standing at the edge of the paved area. "I've got a lettuce for you, and the first tomatoes are ripe. I'll leave them by the back door."

"I'll walk back with you. I've finished here for today."

Jaz re-entered the studio, lifted the cat from the cushion and took him outside. She locked the door and accompanied Ted as he pushed the barrow down the path.

"I had that builder you told me about around earlier," she said.

"Rick? Good bloke. Likes old buildings."

"Yeah, he talked about the house a lot."

"You could do worse." He shot her a meaningful look. "He's single, you know."

"Ted! I'm looking for a builder, not a boyfriend."

"Sure you are." He raised a bushy grey eyebrow, blue eyes twinkling. "But like I said, you could do worse."

She bent to smell a rose hoping he hadn't noticed the blush stealing to her cheeks. "All right, that's enough matchmaking. I can find my own boyfriends."

"I'm sure you can, a gorgeous lass like you, but I'm saving you some time."

"Okay, let's change the subject. Do you know if any alterations have been done to the house?"

Ted brought the wheelbarrow to a stop. "You mean besides the conservatory?"

"Yes. Inside the house."

His eyes scanned the rear elevation of the house. He scratched his head, pondered for a minute. "Not while I've been working here."

"Rick said there's a false wall in the library."

"I don't know anything about that. If there is, it must have been before my time." He started trundling the wheelbarrow again. "I'll ask my mother-in-law if she knows anything. Her family have lived here for centuries and she's a walking encyclopaedia when it comes to local history."

* * *

•

Whisper finished the tuna fish in his bowl, licked his lips and set about washing himself, while Jaz crunched her way through the last of the salad she'd made from Ted's vegetables and the other half of the can of tuna. She rinsed her plate and glass. Not worth using the dishwasher.

Still hungry, she scoured the pantry shelves. Nothing appealed. She wanted something sweet. She checked the fridge. Yoghurt. Her mouth drooped in disappointment. Only one thing would satisfy her craving: chocolate.

The village shop, with its shelves crammed with confectionary, beckoned.

She patted Whisper's head. "I'll be back soon. Be good."

The sun still held some warmth as it headed to bed. Long black shadows crawled across the earth. On the village green, a battle to see who could make most noise ensued between a group of rowdy teenagers and a flock of birds preparing to nest. The birds were winning.

A few minutes later she retraced her steps, happily contemplating the rest of her evening communing with a Walnut Whip and a box of Jaffa Cakes. Yum! She loved Walnut Whips. First she'd pick off the nut, then lick the top until the chocolate melted, giving way to the soft white centre. She'd suck at the sweet goo, then nibble at the chocolate spiral until her tongue flicked out the last of the fondant, leaving only the thick chocolate base to be devoured. She smacked her lips together in anticipation.

"Watch out!"

The sound hit her ears a split second before the boy careened into her, bowling her off her feet. A fleeting glimpse of a skateboard rattling into the gutter tweaked her peripheral vision as she crashed towards the ground. She flung her hands out to break her fall, palms stinging as they hit the gritty road. The breath left her body and her left elbow exploded in agony. Sheets of red, white and black pain fragmented and reformed behind her eyes.

Stunned, she lay on the ground, snatching for air. The contents of her handbag scattered creating a rainbow on the ground.

The boy bent over her. She recognised him: Kieran Black, the butcher's son. "Sorry. I couldn't stop. I'm still learning. Don't tell my dad, will you? He'll kill me."

Dazed, Jaz pushed to a sitting position, and picked the grit from her reddened palms. She flexed her throbbing elbow, it hurt but didn't appear broken. A thin trickle of blood wound down her shin from a graze on her knee.

A shadow fell across her. "Are you all right? Need some help? Oh, it's you."

Silhouetted against the setting sun she couldn't make out the man's features, until he crouched beside her.

She looked into Rick Moran's concerned eyes. Her breath shortened, this time not because she'd been winded by the fall. "He knocked me over."

"You should be more careful on that thing," Rick snarled at Kieran.

Kieran shuffled from foot to foot, hands twisting his beanie. "I said I'm sorry. I'm still learning."

"It's okay, Kieran." Jaz rubbed her elbow; the pain had lessened. "Accidents happen. You can go."

Kieran didn't need telling twice. He grabbed his skateboard, tucked it under his arm and ran across the road and onto the village green.

Rick held out his hand. "Can you stand up?"

"Yes, I'm fine really." She took his hand — warm, strong and welcoming — and let him hoist her to her feet

He looked at her leg. "You're bleeding."

Jaz rubbed at the blood, smearing it. "It's nothing. It's almost stopped. Barely more than a scratch."

She bent over and started collecting the things that had fallen from her bag. Keys, purse, bundle of tissues, eyeliner, half a packet of chewing gum.

Rick retrieved her cell phone, and examined the thick rubber covering. "Your phone's fared better than you. Maybe you should buy a rubber suit."

Jaz snatched the phone, pressed the keys through the clear rubber and checked it worked. "Thanks, it's fine."

Offering no explanation for its unusual covering, she dropped it into her bag, and mentally ticked off her possessions. No lipstick, no screwdriver. She widened her search, scanned the pavement and road and then spotted the grate. She leant over it. Through the slats she saw the lipstick's metallic case lying in the mud at the bottom of the storm drain.

"No! Not my raspberry sorbet lippy!" She'd only bought the luscious colour last week. "Wait till I get my hands on Kieran Black."

To the side of her lipstick she could see the red handle of her screwdriver poking out of the sludge. Until she bought another one she wouldn't be able to drive her car.

"Shit!" She stamped her foot in frustration.

"Are these yours too?" In one hand Rick held the Jaffa Cakes, the corner of the box was dented, but otherwise they looked all right. The same could not be said for the Walnut Whip.

"Oh, no! Not my Walnut Whip." She took the squashed confectionary from his hand, and examined the crush of chocolate and fondant. She must have landed on it when she fell. She'd been so looking forward to eating it, and now that tiny pleasure had been snatched away. Overwhelmed by sadness disproportionate to the event, her jaw trembled and a fat tear dropped onto the back of her hand, followed by another and another.

Try as she might she couldn't stop the tears.

"It's only a Walnut Whip," said Rick, patting her upper arm.

"I kn...know," Jaz wailed. Embarrassed she turned away and dug in her bag for the tissues.

Gently, he turned her back, enfolded her in his arms and held her tight. She sank against him for a moment, not caring that her tears soaked his shirt, just glad to have someone strong to lean on for a minute or two, even if he was a virtual stranger.

"We'll get you another one," he said.

Struck by how ridiculous she was being, a chuckle rose in her throat, spluttering from her mouth as it mixed with her sobs. She straightened up and dabbed at her eyes with the tissue.

"Sorry. I didn't mean to..."

"Don't apologise. I once lost my last Rolo. Cried for a week."

She offered him a weak smile, appreciating his attempt to make light of the situation. "My emotions have been all over the place since my mum died. I cry over the most stupid things."

"That's grief for you. Gets you when you're not expecting it." A shadow fell across his face, and he gazed into the distance. He took a deep breath. "I lost my dad a couple of years ago."

"Grim, isn't it?"

"Yeah, but one day you don't hurt quite so much, and gradually you learn to deal with it. I can even watch football again without getting maudlin. How about your dad? Is he still alive?"

"I've no idea. I'm the product of a holiday romance. Some Italian guy called Mario. Mum met him island hopping in Greece when she was a teenager. She didn't even know his full name."

"Wow. That's tough."

Jaz wrinkled her nose. "Not really. Besides, Ted has always been around if I need a father figure."

"He's a good bloke." His face crinkled into a grin. "How do you fancy a drink?"

In normal circumstances Jaz would be delighted to have a drink with him—or dinner, or a movie, or... the list went on and on. She looked down at her dishevelled clothes and her dirty hands and leg. "I'm a bit of a mess."

"Nothing that can't be sorted. Come on. You could do with a stiff drink after your fall. It's good for shock."

"Maybe I should pop home, clean myself up a bit."

"Nonsense. We've everything we need here." He took her hand and led her to a bench on the green. "Give me a tissue."

She handed him several. While he strode across the green to the ancient well she opened the Jaffa Cakes and bit into one. He dipped some tissues in the water, and brought them back to her. Declining a Jaffa Cake, he lifted her injured leg onto the bench and wiped away the blood.

Beneath the touch of his fingers, Jaz's nerve endings danced in a frenzy of delight. Who needed to go for a drink? She'd be quite happy sat here all night. His hand rested on her thigh as he paused to examine her knee. She let out an involuntary groan of pleasure. He looked up. She stuffed the rest of her biscuit into her mouth, and breaking the cardinal sin of speaking with her mouthful, said, "Oooh, these Jaffa Cakes are soooooo yummy. You should have one."

He smiled, placed her foot back on the ground, and then sat beside her. "You're right, it's nothing more than a graze. Let's see your hands."

Like a gleeful five year old, Jaz swung her legs to and fro while he cleaned her mucky hands. She could have cleaned herself up, but being pampered proved much more fun.

Chapter Three

Discombobulate.

Jaz loved the word, the very sound of it, the way it filled her mouth and rolled around her tongue. She first heard it as a twelve year old and it turned her onto words in a big way. Over the years she'd managed to turn this passion into a capacity for creating crosswords. Her puzzles were in great demand, and allowed her to carve out a career that paid the bills with the flexibility of being able to work to her own timetable. As long as she had access to the Internet she could work anywhere, and still meet her deadlines.

Sat in the shade of the laburnum tree, she set the fourteen-letter word into a blank grid on her laptop screen, and typed the clue. Hidden from her sight in the depths of the herbaceous border, bees buzzed. Whisper chased a butterfly, leaping into the air, claws outstretched. His quarry ducked and dived before twisting above the cat's head and escaping. Jaz settled to her task, losing track of time as she developed the symmetrical pattern, settled on words and created fiendish clues.

The slap-slap-slap of small feet trotting down the path through the rose garden broke her contemplation of the final clue. She looked up, and waved to Ted's little granddaughter. Ted followed; a bundle of beach towels tucked under one arm.

"Jasmy, Jasmy. It's me." Wet ringlets bounced on the girl's shoulders as she ran towards Jaz.

Jaz hit the save icon, set the laptop to one side and rose to her feet.

"Hello, Millie." She bent over, caught the little girl in her arms and swung her round, enjoying the sound of the high-pitched squeals of delight.

Deposited back on the ground, Millie staggered dizzily then plopped onto the grass. "We been swimming in the river. You can go if you want to."

"It's a perfect day for it," said Ted.

"I don't think so." Jaz rubbed the back of her neck, her skin felt sticky with clammy sweat. "It's incredibly muggy. There's a storm coming. I can feel it in my bones."

Ted shook his head. "You shouldn't let that bother you. Don't you know lightning never strikes in the same place twice?"

"That's easy for you to say. You weren't the one with a billion volts shooting through you." She moved her hand to her left shoulder and covered the fernlike scar that marked the entry point of the lightning bolt that had seared its way through her body when she was eighteen. That had been a day much like this, hot, overcast and humid, the air thick and oppressive. Then, like now, the dull throb of a headache threatened at her temple. Desperate to cool down, she'd slipped into her bikini, pulled on an oversize T-shirt and sandals, grabbed a towel and climbed over the stile at the bottom of the garden. Her fingers trailed through the long grass as she crossed the cornflower and poppy littered meadow.

The heat left her body as she plunged from the jetty into the cool running water of the river and swam to the opposite bank where, under the drooping boughs of a weeping willow, she treaded water. In the distance, thunder rumbled. Moving into the centre of the river, Jaz floated on her back and watched the sky darkening. The thunder claps lengthened and intensified as the storm moved closer, frightening her with its sudden proximity.

She swam back to the jetty and climbed the rusting ladder. After towelling the worst of the water from her body, she dressed and draped the towel around her shoulders. As she wiggled her toes into her sandals the clouds broke and rainfall pelted. The crashes of thunder reached a crescendo, overlapping one another, lightning forked, illuminating the meadow for an instant, as though some great celestial camera was taking a photograph.

Jaz loved watching storms from inside the house, but she didn't like this. Her ears rang from the din. She began to run through the premature darkness, staying close to the wire fence at the edge of the meadow. The long grass tugged at her legs impeding her progress. Another few paces and she'd reach the stile, then a mad dash through the garden and she'd be home.

She never made the stile.

She couldn't outrun the lightning.

It struck her with a force like no other. A few milliseconds that lasted an eternity. Most of the current danced over her body surface in an external flashover, but some shot through her shoulder, racing to earth down her length and out through her foot. Her sandals exploded, her clothes shredded, her hair sizzled and her eyebrows burned off. Her silver necklace melted and burnt into her skin.

Somehow she survived, becoming part of an exclusive group of people who managed to live through an encounter with the deadly force.

She awoke in hospital with a fractured collarbone sustained when she fell to the ground. Her big toe nail had vanished. Her other injuries centred on the burns at the entry and exit points, and from the links of her necklace. It had taken her weeks to recover, and she'd been left with a few permanent injuries, including joint stiffness, and bouts of dizziness and weakness. Sometimes she experienced numbness in her hands and her once perfect vision had been affected. She required glasses more and more often.

As she stroked the scar on her shoulder, Jaz shook her head. "I don't swim anymore, Ted. I've forgotten how."

Ted scratched his whiskers. Don't be ridiculous. It's like riding a bike, once learnt you don't forget how."

"I'm not going to chance finding out. I had my last swim a long time ago."

"That's a pity. You swam like a fish when you were a nipper."

"I don't miss it," she lied. "I do other things now instead."

"Jasmy. Can I find strawberries?" Millie tugged at Jaz's shorts. "Gwanddad said I can. Please. Can I?"

"Only if you pick some for me, too."

"I will."

Lethargic in the heat, Jaz marvelled at Millie's energy, as she watched the little girl running through the rose garden. Jaz and Ted sauntered after her.

Ted collected a couple of old margarine tubs from the potting shed, picked a curled up desiccated spider from one and flicked it onto the soil. "I asked my mother-in-law about the house."

Jaz's curiosity piqued. "What did she say? Can she remember any alterations?"

"'Fraid not."

"Damn." *What a let down.* She'd hoped the old woman might have some answers. She kicked at a small stone, watched it scuttle away.

"Don't look so miserable. She does remember something else that you might find interesting."

Jaz brightened. "What?"

"You know, you haven't changed since you were a wee lass, like our Millie. One minute grumpy, the next grinning like a Cheshire Cat."

Millie turned at the sound of her name and smiled. Crouched between the strawberry runners, her cheeks plump and distorted from the mass of fruit she'd squeezed in, she looked like she'd found paradise. Juice dribbled down her chin, staining her cotton dress.

"There's lots of them, Jasmy. Here." She held out a ripe specimen.

Jaz took the red berry and bit into it. "That's delicious, Millie. Yummy."

"Yummy for my tummy." Millie rubbed her belly and chuckled.

"Fill these up, Cheeky Chops." Ted passed her the tubs then turned to Jaz. "That'll keep her quiet for a while. Apparently, your house is built in an interesting spot. Do you know what ley lines are?"

Jaz shook her head. "Never heard of them."

"The name ley is the old Saxon word for meadow. Ley lines connect one ancient site to another. They are considered to be the Earth's natural energy lines. It's also believed that spirits may use these for traveling quickly from one place to another."

She raised a sceptical eyebrow. "You mean spirits like ghosts?"

"If you like. Ghosts, spirits, psychic energy, whatever you want to call them."

"Sorry, I don't believe in all that stuff."

"Don't apologise to me, I'm just telling you what I've been told by Elsie."

"Granddad, look. Look. It's a ladybird." Millie held out a finger to show off the tiny insect. Then she blew on it and clapped her hands as it flew away. "Fly away, fly away, fly away home." She ran around in a circle flapping her arms.

"Watch the strawberries, Millie. Don't go squashing them." She looked down at her half filled tubs then returned to her task.

"Okay, tell me more about these ley lines and why they're so important."

"There's also a theory that electricity flows along the lines." Ted sat down on the edge of a raised vegetable bed and pulled out some chickweed.

"And?"

He looked up and winked at her. "You're going to love this. It appears your house stands on a ley line."

Jaz laughed in disbelief. "You're kidding."

"You don't have to believe it, but you know those stones scattered around the garden?"

"You mean those big rocks?"

"Yes. They're part of a stone circle."

"I think I knew that." Jaz twisted a lock of hair round her index finger, and chewed her lip. Since the lightning strike she had gaps in her memory, but every now and again something came back. She concentrated hard, teasing the recollection, drawing it from the dark recesses of her mind until daylight dawned and she remembered. "Yes, I did, Ted. I remember. Nannalu and Grandma Faye told me about that. It's probably been here since the Bronze Age, but some of the stones are missing."

"Do you remember anything else?"

Her gaze travelled round the garden, spotting the standing stones. For millennia the limestone rocks had stood on this land, silent sentinels. Nobody knew why they'd been put there. She looked at the house.

"There are some more stones," she remembered. "Round the sides and front of the house. They make up what's left of the circle. The house is built inside the stone circle, isn't it?"

Ted stood up, wiped his hands on his trousers. "Yes, it's slap bang in the middle."

"Why did they build it there?"

"Perhaps they thought it would have mystical properties. Or maybe because the view's so lovely from here. We'll probably never know, after all it is over two hundred years old."

Jaz frowned. "I'm surprised they were allowed to build inside the circle."

"I'm not. They owned the land. Up to them what they did with it."

"They wouldn't have been allowed to build at Stonehenge."

Ted laughed. "It's hardly on the same scale. Your biggest stone is only a metre tall."

"So what? It's an ancient site, it should have been preserved."

"It has been. Now there's a house in the middle of it. That's all."

"It's odd." She wandered over to Millie. "Wow. Look at all those strawberries. You've done a good job."

Millie beamed. Jaz picked up the tubs and passed one to Ted. "We're going to have a good lunch with these, aren't we?"

"I want ice-cream with mine," said Millie.

"That's a good idea. We'll buy some at the shop on the way home," said Ted, taking his granddaughter's hand in his and leading the way back through the garden. She skipped at his side.

When they approached the vine-clad studio, Ted stopped and turned to Jaz. "There is another reason the house may have been built here."

"What?" Jaz popped a perfect strawberry from her tub into her mouth, biting down on the sweetness.

"Apparently your house was built over a well. Presumably so the occupants didn't have to go outside for water. The house was built long before people had indoor plumbing."

"I know that." Jaz looked at the house. "What happened to the well?"

Ted shrugged. "My mother-in-law was told about the well when she was a girl, but she never saw it. It may have been a rumour or maybe it was filled in when the water supply arrived. A big house like this was probably the first in the village to get modern utilities."

His gaze roamed across the weathered stone flagstones outside the studio. "It may even have been in one of these outbuildings. Makes sense with that stone trough being there."

"I wonder if the original plans still exist? There are so many dusty old books in the library they could easily be on a shelf. They're the sort of thing my great-granddad would have kept. Ooh, I feel a treasure hunt coming on."

Chapter Four

"The trouble with libraries..." Jaz told Whisper, running her finger across the spines of several volumes as she balanced on the stepladder. "...is they're full of books."

From his observation post on the Turkish rug, Whisper mewed in sympathy, then rolled onto his back, enjoying the warm shaft of sunlight filtering through the windows.

"And the trouble with books is they're full of words. Lovely words that distract me from my purpose." She pulled out a couple of heavy tomes, hefted them into her arms, climbed down the ladder and dropped them on the desk beside the dozen she'd already sifted through. She caressed the cracked leather cover of an oversized volume and sighed. "At this rate I'm going to be here for weeks."

The phone rang. Jaz leapt over Whisper, dashed into the hallway and grabbed the receiver on the fourth ring.

"Hello."

"Hi, Jaz. It's Eva." For the last few months Jaz had been continuing her dance lessons as one of Eva's students. "I need a big favour. Are you busy tonight?"

"That depends on what you want." Looking at her reflection in the mirror above the hall table, Jaz noticed a zit on her chin. Where had that come from? Her skin had been clear when she got ready this morning.

"Sarah's got toothache. She's in agony, poor thing. The dentist says she needs a root canal, but he can't do it until tomorrow. There's no way she can dance tonight."

"And?" The zit appeared to grow before Jaz's eyes. Nasty red blob, making her skin taut and shiny, and the white head looked about to erupt.

"And I was wondering if you could fill in for her," Eva wheedled.

"Why me? Is nobody else available?"

Eva laughed. "I don't know, but you're my first choice."

Wow! First choice. Since she'd only been dancing with the troupe for a few months she couldn't believe Eva thought she was ready to do a show. Especially a last minute one. "Really?"

"Look, you know all the dances, and your solo is almost perfected. It'll be a good opportunity to perform before an audience."

Jaz hadn't performed in public in well over a year, and a knot of nervousness fluttered in her stomach. "Who's the show for?"

"Some bloke's fortieth birthday. His wife thought he'd enjoy it. Please say you'll do it. It'll be fun."

"My costume's not finished." The zit grew before her eyes.

"You can borrow my red one if you like. Or my turquoise and silver. Please say yes."

Jaz considered the offer. Eva was right, she did know the choreographies, she'd thrashed them until she knew them backwards, but as she looked at her pasty skin and lank hair she felt anything but confident. Eva was more than an inspirational teacher. She looked like a goddess when she danced, and Jaz didn't want to let her down. "I'm flattered, really I am, and I'd love to do it, but it's so long since I've done a show. I'm not ready."

"You'll be fine. I'll pop round about half past six and we can do a quick run through. They don't want us to dance until eight thirty, so we'll have plenty of time."

"I haven't said yes yet."

"It's only a matter of time before you agree, so let's pretend we've had that conversation and you're going to do it."

"You're twisting my words." Jaz fingered her zit and winced. "I've got a spot the size of Vesuvius on my chin."

"Pop it! Cover it in makeup. Stick a bindi on it. I don't care. Say you'll come."

Absently, Jaz began doing hip circles. "Okay, you win. I'll do it."

"Fantastic! You're a lifesaver. Which costume do you want me to bring?"

"I'll let you know if I need one. I'll try to finish mine. It's almost done."

"See you at six thirty."

Jaz hung up the phone. She moved closer to the mirror, put her index fingers on either side of the uninvited guest and evicted it.

* * *

The sequins on Jaz's costume sparkled, and the chiffon layers of her skirt lifted and fluttered in the breeze from the open window. Since Eva's phone call she'd worked like a machine. First, she'd completed the last section of sequins along her bra straps, and then stitched the beaded fringing along the bottom edge.

The costume completed to her satisfaction, she hung it on the wardrobe door while she set to work on herself. Defuzzing her arms and legs, plucking eyebrows into a perfect arch, covering herself top to bottom with bronzing powder and realising she needed to be a contortionist to get that bit of her back above the centre of her bra strap. She'd have to get Eva to do that section when she arrived.

With the help of her hair straighteners she coaxed her hair into loose curls, and scooped one side behind her ear fixing it in place with a sparkly slide. With practised hands she glued her false eyelashes into place, fluttered them, looked in the mirror and grinned. The transformation from plain old Jaz into Aisha, the Middle Eastern belly dancer, neared completion. She applied her makeup: defining her cheekbones, further emphasising her eyes with heavy black kohl, and creating a perfect red pout.

She heard the tinkle of Whisper's little bell, and the patter of his paws as he trotted along the landing. He poked his head around the bedroom door.

"Hello. Have you been playing out?"

Whisper rubbed his head up and down the edge of the door, and then jumped onto the bed, walking around and around in circles before settling down to sleep.

From her collection of nail varnish Jaz chose an emerald green that matched her skirt. She painted two coats onto her toe and fingernails, and finished with a layer of silver sparkles. Whilst her nails dried she listened to the music for her solo, visualising the sensuous hip moves and cheeky bust pops. She hoped she'd be able to remember it. If not, she'd have to improvise. As long as she kept moving and smiling she'd be fine.

As soon as her nails dried she wriggled into her costume, checking her panties couldn't be seen through the layers of delicate fabric. The uplift bra created a splendid cleavage and the beaded fringe swayed tantalisingly as she moved. She fastened the matching hip belt in place, using safety pins on the inside to attach it to her skirt. Normally, to avoid any misadventure during the actual performance, she'd wear the costume in a rehearsal. Tonight she had no such luxury, and prayed nothing would come undone.

Finally, Jaz surveyed her reflection in the full-length mirror. She hardly recognised herself. The grubby young woman in the cut-off jeans, with scabby knee and bruised elbow had vanished. The floor skimming skirt covered her knee, and she'd disguised the bruise and her scars with makeup. An elaborate jewelled necklace glittered at her throat, stacks of silver bangles clinked on her wrists, and dangly earrings flashed whenever she tossed her hair. She turned from side to side, checking each facet, then pleased with her appearance, she did a couple of quick hip twists and watched the beaded fringe whip out and back in a flurry of colour and light. She shimmied on the spot to the pulsating rhythms of the doumbek. It spoke to her soul and she filled with the joy of the dance. Nothing made her as happy or made her feel more alive than twisting and undulating as she tried to interpret the music with her body. She liked what she saw as she watched her reflection—the epitome of a belly dancer.

"We're going to knock 'em dead tonight, Whisper."

He looked at her, but made no comment.

The doorbell rang, loud and summonsing. Jaz glanced at the clock, almost twenty past six.

"Ooh, she's early." She took one last look in the mirror, grabbed the embroidered velvet coat she used as a cover-up for travelling to and from performances and ran downstairs. Whisper overtook her halfway down, and she had to skip to the side to avoid tripping over him as they raced for the door. He reached the hall first and sat with his head cocked waiting to greet the visitor. She hooked the coat over the newel post and flung open the front door.

"Do I pass muster?" She lifted her arms and posed. Then stopped dead.

"Oh, yes. Very nice." The smile on Rick's face couldn't have been wider, or his eyes brighter.

Flustered, her cheeks burning with embarrassment, Jaz jumped backwards and pushed the door closed. She grabbed the coat and tried to put it on, then found one sleeve was inside out from last time she'd worn it. She righted the sleeve, and managed to slip into it. All fingers and thumbs, she struggled to fasten the buttons. Giving up she wrapped the coat tightly around her middle, pinning it in position with one arm.

She took a deep breath, plastered a smile on her face and reopened the door. He'd crouched down, stroking Whisper beneath the chin. "Rick, how lovely to see you."

"Not half as nice as it was to see you." He stood up, eyeing her attire. "No need to cover up for me."

She pulled the coat tighter around her waist, shy at his attention. After their drink last night, he'd walked her home, but made no attempt to kiss her, much as she wanted him to.

He ran a hand through his thick sandy hair, dusty from his day at work. "Are you off to a fancy dress party?"

People's reactions varied when they discovered her passion. Whether they approved or not they always reassessed their opinion of her. She wondered what Rick would say. Only one way to find out. "No, I'm a belly dancer. When I dance I'm called Aisha." She smiled, watching his eyebrows rise. "I'm performing tonight. I thought you were my dance partner."

"Well, Aisha, if you dance half as good as you look your audience is in for a treat."

Her heart shimmied. She glowed with pleasure and slid into dance posture—abs engaged, ribcage lifted—and then, knowing she looked her best, she released her grip on the coat allowing the edges to slip apart revealing a slither of sequins, beads and flesh.

He looked her up and down, then laughed. "You're full of surprises, aren't you?"

"I've one or two up my sleeves." She arched her eyebrows. "Now are you coming in?"

"I'd love to. Seriously, I would, but I'm covered in muck. I came to drop off the quotes." He handed her an envelope, her name written by hand in bold print across the middle. "If there's anything that's not clear give me a call..." There was that grin again. "...And if you're dressed like that you can call anytime. Absolutely anytime. Don't hesitate to pick up the phone."

The scrunch of tyres on gravel saved her replying. Eva's car juddered up the driveway.

He glanced over his shoulder. Turning back to her, he smiled. "I'll be off then."

"Don't you want to meet Eva?"

"If she looks anywhere near as sexy as you my poor heart couldn't stand it." He patted his chest, winked at her, and left.

Tall and blonde, Eva hitched up her skirt to keep the hem from trailing on the ground as she picked her way across the gravel. "Who's the hunk?"

"The builder."

"He must have thought it was his lucky day when he saw you dressed like that. I hope he offered you a discount." Eva laughed as she watched his van drive away, before following Jaz into the house. "So, you managed to finish your bedlah then?"

"Yes, I'm delighted with it." She put the envelope on the table, shrugged out of her coat and did a twirl.

"It's fab. You look stunning."

"You too. That magenta is definitely your colour. I love it."

Eva preened and wiggled her slender hips. "It is gorgeous, isn't it? But I've had to pad the bra quite a bit. You're so lucky with that cleavage."

"Ah, you can't have it both ways. These boobs come with thunder thighs. With your skinny pins you can wear skirts slit to your armpits. Lucky thing."

Eva laughed. "Okay, enough of the mutual admiration society, let's run through the order and have a quick rehearsal." She pulled a CD from her bag. "Here's the music."

"Let's go into the lounge. I've got a couple of fans cooling the room down."

By the time they'd finished the almost flawless practice, Jaz's confidence had built, and she felt ready for the challenge of a human audience. Whisper had his moments, but his feedback needed work.

"I'm staying at my sister's tonight." Eva touched up her lipstick in the hall mirror. "She lives in the opposite direction, so do you mind taking your own car."

"No, that's fine." Jaz sprayed a cloud of perfume in the air and arms aloft walked through the mist. She picked up her coat. "It's so hot. I can hardly bear to put this on. I'll be all sweaty by the time we arrive."

"I know, I thought the storm would have broken by now. But look on the bright side, at least our hair won't get messed up in the wind and rain. Ready?"

"Let's go." Jaz slid on her bejewelled sandals and collected her handbag. "Oh, no! My screwdriver."

"Screwdriver? Why do you need a screwdriver? We're going dancing, not to a joinery class."

"I use it to start my car. The key broke. Last night the screwdriver fell down a drain. Damn Kieran Black and his bloody skateboard."

"No worries. I can bring you back."

"No, it's miles out of your way. There must be something I can use." She ran into the kitchen, yanked open drawer after drawer, rifling through the utensils, but finding nothing that would serve her purpose.

"Jaz, if we don't go, we'll be late."

"Sorry, I meant to buy one today, but then I didn't go out."

"You could get a new key cut, you know."

"Too late for that. I don't know where I put the broken key." Jaz stopped in her tracks. "Oh, I know what might work. Hang on a sec."

Skirt swirling, she dashed into the library. The letter opener stood in a ceramic jar filled with pens and pencils. She took it from the pot, and examined its pointed end; it bore a few small nicks. "The end's not quite the same as the screwdriver, but it's close. It's worth a shot."

"Let me look at that thing." Eva grabbed it and held it up to the light. "It's quite heavy. What is it?"

"A letter opener."

"Fanciest letter opener I've ever seen."

"Is it?" Jaz took it back and looked at it properly. The engraved circular handle, made from gold coloured metal was embedded with pieces of coloured glass. Maybe it was unusual. She didn't know. She'd not seen that many letter openers. "I believe it belonged to my great-grandfather. Something he picked up on his travels. It's always been in the library. I hardly ever use it; I rip the envelopes open with my fingers. It'll be far more use as a car starter, if it works, that is."

Jaz looked around for Whisper, but couldn't see him, so she called farewell and followed Eva outside. Settled into the driving seat, her skirt smoothed beneath her bottom so it wouldn't crease and the rest piled on her lap, she pushed the letter opener into the slot.

"It fits," she called through the open door to Eva.

"Try turning it."

Fingers crossed, Jaz said a little prayer, and then turned the ornate handle. The engine spluttered into life and caught first time. Music blared from the radio. Jubilant, she turned the volume down. "Who needs a key? You go first, I'll follow."

Chapter Five

The show had been a tremendous success. Jaz missed a couple of cues, but her improvisational skills had improved enough for her to fluff her way through without the audience being aware of any mistakes. *Smile and shimmy* became her mantra.

The enthusiastic crowd clapped along to the rhythms of the Arabic music and smiled encouragement. Some of them even joined in at the end, doing their own versions of hip flicks and snake arms. Eva gave her card to two women who wanted lessons, and a man who said he was organising a work function and thought *A Night in Egypt* would be a good theme. All in all a good result.

Home again, Jaz poured a glass of chilled white wine, and took a cool shower. She wrapped her hair in a turban, slipped on a loose cotton robe and went to the kitchen to replenish her glass. Restless, she wandered from room to room, straightening a picture here, running her fingers over a dusty surface there. With only Whisper for company the house seemed too big. She wished her mother was here. She wanted to tell her about her evening, share her happiness about her successful solo.

She drifted upstairs, stopping on the wide landing for a few minutes in front of the display cabinet to examine Nanalu's collection of glass bottles. The fascinating mixture of the ancient and the rare twinkled beneath the soft lights; amidst the beautiful specimens resided a few ugly vessels. She couldn't understand why Nanalu had wanted those, but she supposed they must have some value, even if it was only through age.

Whisper sat on the landing, poking his head between the barley twist rails, and watching the shadow of a moth as it flitted around the hallway. When Jaz moved along the landing past her bedroom he followed.

She took the narrow stairs to the attics and opened the door into her mother's room. A wall of heat met her. Despite her recent shower a thin sheen of sweat already coated her. She put her wine glass on the bedside table and switched on the lamp, before crossing to the dormer window and flinging it open. Hoping for a breeze, she stuck her head out, only to be disappointed by the cloying air, thick with the scent of night stocks even at this height.

Whisper flopped onto the carpet.

Jaz flopped onto the bed. "I know how you feel, but I admit it's probably worse for you with that thick fur coat."

She looked around the room, trying to understand her mother's affinity with the attics. Something to do with the light and the angles of the sloping ceilings and the exposed beams. Maybe only an artist would get it. Jaz much preferred the bedrooms on the floor below, with their perfect proportions, ornate cornices and deep skirting boards. Still, her mother had turned her artistic eye to this room when decorating, the result a sumptuous mix of rich colour and tactile fabrics. Everything in the room screamed out Theresa's name and it comforted Jaz not to change a thing, but to let her mother's presence live on in this space.

The carved oak bed nestled against the wall. She sat up and plumped the pillows, rearranging them so she could lean in the corner of the headboard and wall, wallowing in the atmosphere whilst she finished her wine.

Whisper jumped onto the bed, tried to sit on her lap, but she pushed him away. "Sorry, mate. It's too hot."

After a second failed attempt, he settled by her side.

The high excitement of the night wore off, as the wine began to act in much the same manner as Mr McGregor's lettuces had on Peter Rabbit. She yawned, then drained her glass and put it down. Tugging the turban off her head, she tossed the towel across the room onto the bedding box, and let her damp hair cascade down her back, enjoying the coolness where it touched her skin.

"I'm going to sleep here tonight. Would you like to join me?" She ran her fingers through Whisper's fur, and he began to purr.

A stack of books sat on the table by the wine glass. Her mother always had several on the go at once. What she read depended on her mood. Jaz glanced at the titles and selected a dog-eared copy of Stephen King's *Misery*. A grubby bookmark with a cross-stitched design of pansies marked her mother's place. As an eleven year old, Jaz had spent weeks embroidering the scrap of fabric, pricking her fingers, and unpicking mistakes, but the look of delight on her mother's face when she opened the birthday gift made her efforts worthwhile. Touched that the bookmark was still in use, Jaz almost choked on a bubble of raw emotion as it charged up her gullet. It spluttered from her mouth as tears sprang from her eyes. She let them roll for a minute, pressing the bookmark to her lips. Her mother would never use it again, never smile at it fondly, never touch it, never touch Jaz, and she'd never, ever finish *Misery* or any of the other books she'd been reading before the accident. She keened out her sadness, tears raced down her cheeks and dripped onto her chest where they formed a little puddle.

Whisper stood, he pushed his head under her hand, rubbing it from side to side, and miaowed. Vision blurred, she looked at his dear little face, his big green eyes full of concern.

"I'm okay." She dried the tears with the edge of her robe. "I'm fine. Don't worry about me."

She ruffled his fur, and spotting an opportunity he sat on her lap. Carefully, so as not to disturb him and have his claws come out, she wiggled down the bed until she was in a comfortable reading position. She opened the book and began to read as Whisper repositioned himself on her stomach. Absently, she stroked his back as she lost herself in the novel. Gripped by the story she tried to keep reading, but her eyelids drooped. She read the same sentence half a dozen times, but couldn't make any sense of it. The book fell from her hand with a gentle thud.

She jerked her eyes open, picked up the book and found her place, tried to read the sentence again, but her eyes didn't want to focus on the words. She looked up, caught her image in the long mirror mounted on the wardrobe door. Whisper's tail flicked occasionally on her thigh, but she couldn't see his body. The reflection of the wall shimmered. She blinked a few times. It still looked to be vibrating.

Weird.

She twisted away and looked at the wall. The pattern on the wallpaper did look to be moving.

She rubbed her eyes. Too much wine.

The taffeta curtains billowed out, snapping as a sudden wind raced into the room announcing the arrival of the long awaited storm. Rain beat against the open windowpane, rattling the glass, splattering the sill. A waft of cool air sprinted up her body.

"At last. Exactly what we need. A good storm to wash the world clean."

A resounding clap of thunder boomed. It came so fast one crash overlapped another. Lightning blazed. Shadows climbed the walls. Startled from his sleep Whisper jumped up, back arched, mouth snarling, claws piercing Jaz's stomach. She screamed. He screeched. He leapt forward. A patch of paper dissolved and he disappeared into the wall.

"Whisper!" Jaz couldn't believe her eyes. He'd been sucked into the wall. Not possible. Solid stone. Cats don't disappear into solid stone walls. But he had. He'd gone. She'd seen it with her own eyes.

She scrambled to her knees, pawing at the wall where Whisper had been consumed. Solid. Rock solid.

She tore at the wallpaper, managed to get her fingernails under one edge and ripped it away. She clawed at the plaster, finger tips raw dripping blood on the bed.

All the while, the storm raged on, centred over her house. The door slammed shut, furniture rattled, pictures lifted on their hooks and slapped back onto the walls. Vaguely she was aware of an ornament blowing off the dresser and smashing.

"Give me back my cat, you fucker!" She pounded the wall with her fists. "Give him back to me!"

Once again the room flooded with lightning. The wall gave way beneath her onslaught. Her hands and forearms sank into the stone. She heard the faint sound of Whisper whimpering. Without a thought for her safety, she thrust her head into the space between her arms and using her hands she yanked herself into the darkness. The wall accommodated her, sucking her inwards, oozing around her, and moving her onwards peristalsicly.

Chapter Six

The cold, solid blackness squeezed Jaz tight, scratching at her exposed skin with its sandpaper rough surface. It crushed her chest. Light-headed she fought for oxygen. Precious little existed and she feared she'd suffocate. She wanted to call to Whisper, to offer reassurance, but she hadn't enough breath to utter a sound.

The darkness, so dense she couldn't see her hand in front of her face, left her disoriented. She'd no idea in which direction she faced, but knew she was being twisted and turned.

The motion sped up. Faster and faster. Swirling and twirling. Vomit rose in her throat as travel sickness reared its head. If she threw up she might end up with it over her face, in her eyes. She swallowed hard, forcing the burning concoction back down.

Whisper's pitiful mewing got louder. Closer.

Every one of her muscles protested. Unconsciousness beckoned. She almost succumbed, but didn't. She might not wake up again, might die here in this hellhole. Never be found.

Her guts clenched and cramped, as terror gripped. What if she couldn't get out of here? What a fool she'd been to plunge in headlong, with no idea of what awaited.

Her lungs burned and her head swam, her eyes closed. She could hold on no longer. Self-pity engulfed her as she thought how short her life had been. She forced her eyes open, looking at the dark sides of the tunnel.

She could see.

A pale green light offered hope. Air found its way towards her. She gulped at it, breath after grateful breath. Aided by the tunnel's efforts to expel her headfirst she pulled herself towards the light.

Jaz used her hands to break her fall as she slithered down a smooth wall and landed on the ground. She righted herself, and sat with her back against the wall as she surveyed the space and waited to see if the ground moved. Whisper mewed. She spotted him, cowering in a corner. He'd made himself as small as possible, his paws tucked under his body, head sunk low. Her heart lurched.

"Poor little thing." She crawled towards him staying in contact with the wall, making what she hoped were comforting noises to a cat's ears.

She bent down to his eye level, and stroked his head. "I'm here, Whisper. We'll get out of here." She sounded more confident than she felt. "Wherever here is."

Sitting up, she scooped him onto her lap, checked he hadn't been physically damaged, and stroked him, finding the action helped to soothe her too. Her nose wrinkled against the smell, stale air mixed with something rotting. The green light seeped from the ground and as her eyes grew accustomed to it, she realised she was in a narrow room. One of the longer walls consisted of rough bricks held together with grey mortar. The other three had a smooth finish, around the bottom was a skirting board.

Jaz gasped. She'd know that skirting board anywhere. It matched the ones in her house perfectly. Still clutching Whisper to her chest, she pressed her back against the wall and pushed herself to her feet.

"We're still in the house, Whisper. This must be the bricked up space behind the library wall. Rick was right."

Employing caution, she tiptoed around the edge of the room. She skirted the hole in the ground. A circular hole, almost a metre in diameter. She peered into it and shuddered. She couldn't see the bottom, but the sides glowed with a strange phosphorescence providing the weak illumination.

"Looks like we've found the well. That saves a ton of research. Why would anybody put a well in a library, Whisper? My ancestors must have been nuts. No wonder they bricked it up." She wrinkled her nose. "It doesn't smell too good either, does it?"

She edged past it, then stopped short. On the ground, halfway between the well and the far wall, stood a single glass bottle. Whisper wiggled from her arms and dropped to the ground. He circled the bottle, stopped to sniff it and turned to Jaz. He miaowed and sat by the vessel. Filled with wonder, she knelt beside him.

"This is the missing bottle. Nanalu's treasure. How the hell did it get in here?"

She thought she heard a noise rumble in the bowels of the well. A snake of dread rippled down her spine. "Come on, Whisper. We need to find a way out of here."

She'd no idea how.

Whisper seemed to have forgotten his trauma. He looked content gazing at the bottle. The blue and orange colours inside danced in the light, quite mesmerising. Jaz dragged her eyes away and began examining the walls, but her gaze drifted back to the bottle time and again. She could understand Whisper's fascination with the delightful object. No wonder it had been the pride of Nanalu's collection. She tried to concentrate on the task at hand. They had to find an exit, but the only way out she cold see was the way in. The hole in the wall gaped, the edges pulsing as though they were alive. God, she didn't want to go back in there. Her heart raced remembering the claustrophobic tunnel, but she had no choice. They could go back in the tunnel and hope it spewed them out on her mother's bed, or they could sit here until they starved to death. If she died first, would Whisper eat her flesh? It didn't bare thinking about.

"I'm sorry, Whisper. It's the only way."

He resisted as she picked him up, but she ignored his claws. If leaving the bottle upset him, wait till he realised where he was going.

Chapter Seven

The dawn chorus burst forth with a rendition worthy of a choir of rock divas. Whisper sprang to the floor, stretched and strutted from the room. Jaz groaned, her head throbbed. How could birds be so chirpy, upbeat and noisy at such an ungodly hour? Didn't they know it was still the middle of the night? She buried her head under the pillow, wishing Whisper would hurry up and chase the rowdy rabble away.

The birdsong rose to a crescendo. Still half asleep, Jaz hurled her pillow towards the window, then flopped back onto the bed. Not wanting to be awake she screwed her eyes tight shut against the early morning light. What she wanted was to return to her dream in which she was stepping into the shower where Rick waited with a bar of scented soap.

She tried to recapture the dream to no avail. Rick slipped away. The cacophonous birds had won, and the new day beckoned. She rubbed the sleep from her eyes and stretched. Her body ached from head to toe. As she lay adjusting to the day, she remembered her other dream. The nightmare. It forced itself into her mind making her quiver as she recalled her rampant fear. It had seemed so real. Stone walls dissolving. Silly. She rolled onto her side and looked at the wall and rapped on it.

"Ouch!" Her knuckles stung, her hand recoiled. She examined her fingers, gasped at the scratches, the broken nails and chipped nail varnish. Had she raked at the wall in her dream? She stared at it; the paper didn't appear to be torn, in fact, looked perfect. She ran her fingertips down her arms, over her body, wincing at the tenderness of her flesh. She flung off the sheet and loosened her robe, revealing countless small grazes and bruises littering her skin. Smears of dried blood adorned the sheets. She clutched her throat. Not a dream.

Reality!

Her gaze riveted to the wall, Jaz leapt from the bed, and backed up until she bumped into the wardrobe. She remembered battling with Whisper, as he squirmed and clawed, trying to resist being pushed back into the tunnel. Through sheer force of will she'd managed to shove him into the gap, which grabbed onto him, sucking him forward, upwards into the darkness. Equally afraid, she followed, knowing she had no other option. The confined space had pummelled her as the blackness became complete. Her head thumped and her chest constricted as once more she fought for air. She must have passed out because she couldn't remember being ejected from the wall, or landing back on the bed, but somehow she and Whisper had survived.

Heart racing, Jaz inched her way from the room, slammed the door behind her and charged down the stairs and into the bathroom. She locked the door, and leant against it catching her breath, listening for strange noises, hearing none. Then standing in front of the mirror she turned from side to side, checking out the full extent of her wounds. Raw red flesh peeked through the ragged slivers of pale skin hanging loosely over her grazes. She cringed touching the grey and yellow bruises on her hips and thighs. Patinaed in white dust she looked none too pretty, but at least she'd incurred no serious injuries.

She ran the bath, added some scented oil and sank into its depths. As she gently sponged the grime off her face, arms and legs and tried to make sense of the night's events, Whisper scratched at the door.

"I won't be long," she said.

"Miaow, miaow." Accompanied by more scratching.

"I'm in the bath. You'll have to wait."

His mewing became more pitiful, his scratching more urgent, and Jaz relented. He must be jittery too. As she let him in he rubbed against her shins, threading his way between her legs and purring. She relocked the door, climbed back into the bath and added more hot water.

"Scary night, eh?"

"Miaow." Whisper sat on the bathmat and washed behind his ears.

Jaz nibbled on a broken nail trying to blunt and shape the sharp edge whilst mulling over her options. She could sit in the bath all day, but eventually she'd be hungry. Or she could face whatever waited for her beyond the door. Neither option appealed. "What should we do next?"

Whisper glanced at the closed door.

"I suppose you're right. No point being a wimp."

● * *
●

Daylight flooded the house as Jaz opened the curtains in room after room. Suddenly the house lost its power to scare her. The furniture, artefacts and ornaments of her family surrounded reassured her and provided a sense of safety. Ascending the stairs, she ran her hand along the banister, worn smooth by decades of touch. She remembered how, when her mother wasn't watching, she used to slide down it. Funny how one day she'd stopped doing it. Like running everywhere. Once upon a time she found it almost impossible to walk anywhere, whether down the garden, to the shop, or along the corridors at school. Now, she rarely ever ran. Last time was when she hurtled through the hospital, almost colliding with a patient on a trolley, as she tried to reach her dying mother's bedside.

She hovered on the landing outside the attics, then pressed her ear to the door of her mother's room. No sound.

Perhaps she should find a weapon just in case. She considered retrieving the ornamental sword she sometimes used for dancing, but dismissed the idea. A blunt sword could offer no protection against a wall that had the ability to swallow her whole. She took a deep breath and turned the doorknob. She'd survived once, she could survive again.

The room looked exactly as she'd left it. Splayed open on the floor, spine upwards, some of its pages creased, lay *Misery*. She picked it up and prodded the wall with the corner of the book half expecting it to be snatched from her hand. Nothing happened. She straightened the creased pages, placed the book on the cabinet, and stripped the bloodstained sheets from the bed. Pieces of the fractured ornament were scattered across the carpet. She dropped them in the wastepaper basket, closed the window, and with the bundle of sheets under her arm left the room.

Whatever had happened in there last night was beyond comprehension. Nobody would believe her, except, maybe...

Grandma Faye!

Jaz dumped the sheets on the kitchen table, and picked up the phone, hitting speed dial. Impatient, she danced from foot to foot as she waited for her maternal grandmother to answer.

Grandma Faye had always been on the periphery of Jaz's life, having spent much of her own life overseas. At a time when women had limited opportunities, Faye ignored convention. With the full support of her mother, she chose to challenge the male-dominated climate towards female reporters, and set off to forge a career as an overseas correspondent. Her work had taken her to some of the scariest places on earth. Intrepid and ingenious, she managed to be first on the scene at disaster after disaster, filing her stories ahead of her rivals.

In the early sixties, when she married photographer Grant Sinclair, everyone expected her to resign, but Faye could no more give up her exhilarating work than she could stop breathing. The only respite came when she gave birth to twins:

Jaz's mother, Theresa, and her Uncle Brendon. Brendon had emigrated to New Zealand when Jaz was three and she'd only seen him twice since then. Grant had died in a plane crash as his twins approached adolescence, and Jaz knew him only from photographs and the odd anecdote or two.

Since their earliest days the twins had been raised by Nanalu. Jaz's mother had confided that Nanalu hated giving up her career after marriage and had lived vicariously through Faye's pursuits, revelling in her daughter's success. Faye and Grant would return home between assignments, doting on their offspring for a few short days, before itchy feet and the lure of new horizons catapulted them into another adventure. Theresa hated being abandoned by her parents.

When she reached eighteen, to celebrate the end of the school year, she and her friends holidayed in Turkey. Within days she'd left her inhibitions behind and fallen for the charms of a young labourer. Back home she discovered that besides the cheap tourist tat she'd purchased, she'd have a permanent souvenir of her trip. Her efforts to track down the labourer proved fruitless and she resigned herself to single parenthood. When Jaz was born Theresa swore she'd not work outside the home but dedicate herself to raising her child, and provide the baby with the mother she'd always wanted for herself. The mother Faye had never been.

A voice, gravelly from decades of smoking, answered the phone. "Jasmine, is that you? Is something wrong?"

"No, Grandma. Well, not wrong exactly."

"Couldn't it wait till morning?"

"It is morning."

"Not here it's not. It's four a.m. for God's sake."

Jaz hadn't thought about the time difference. It was impossible to keep up with where her grandmother was anyway. At seventy-two, she showed little sign of slowing down, still the perennial globetrotter. "Sorry, shall I call back later?"

"No, I'm awake now." Jaz heard a match striking, then her grandma drawing on a cigarette. "What do you want?"

"Has the house ever done anything strange?"

"What do you mean, strange?"

Tongue-tied, Jaz had no idea how to put into words what had happened. She'd sound like a total loony.

"Jasmine, don't tell me you've woken me up in the middle of the goddamn night for nothing. Spit it out, girl." Grandma Faye could never be accused of mollycoddling.

"I know this sounds weird, but... it's like this..."

"Jasmine!"

"Sorry. It's..." Jaz twisted the telephone cord round and round.

Faye sighed. Jaz could hear her drumming her fingers against the phone.

She screwed up her eyes, wishing she'd not bothered calling. "Last night the wall in the attic dissolved and dragged Whisper into its depths, then me."

"What?"

Jaz forced herself to carry on. "The wall sucked my cat in, then me and we ended up in a room that's hidden behind the bookshelves in the library."

"Are you on drugs?"

"No! I knew you wouldn't believe me."

"Well, who's ever heard of dissolving walls? That house is as solid as a rock."

"That's what I thought."

"You must have been dreaming."

"That's what I thought." Jaz repeated in a whisper, looking at the scratches on her hands and arms.

Her grandma's voice softened. "You've been under a lot of strain since your mum died. Maybe you should see a doctor."

Jaz had no intention of seeing a doctor. Judging by her grandma's reaction she'd probably end up being committed to an insane asylum. No thank you. She'd manage on her own.

"You will go and see the doctor, won't you?"

"Uhuh." Grandma could interpret that however she liked.

"I'll be back next month. We can go away together if you like. Somewhere nice. Now, if there's nothing else I'm going to try and get some sleep. Goodnight."

Jaz returned the receiver to its cradle. Grandma Faye had obviously not experienced anything odd here. Maybe nobody else had. Certainly nobody had ever mentioned anything about secret tunnels. Ooh, a secret passage, like in the Enid Blyton books she'd devoured as a child. She'd always wanted a house like that.

Her spirit brightened. She put the sheets in the washing machine with a generous scoop of powder, and set the dial. Water gurgled through the pipes, as she popped some bread into the toaster and made a pot of coffee. She opened the window, letting in air, fresh after the storm. The garden had taken a battering. Bright yellow laburnum blossoms, mixed with pink and purple petals from the herbaceous border, carpeted the lawn. She hoped the strawberries had survived.

The shrill ring of the phone broke into her thoughts.

"Hello."

"Good morning, Jaz. It's Annabel Harrington." Annabel's private school accent sounded even plummier over the phone. "Wasn't last night's storm amazing?"

Jaz looked at her damaged hands, with their chipped varnish and broken nails, and remembered Annabel's perfect manicure. "That's one way of putting it. I swear it was centred on the house. The thunder claps rolled into one another."

"How thrilling! All that power and energy being unleashed. Don't you love a good storm?"

"Not so much." She stroked the scar on her shoulder. "To tell the truth, I'm a bit of a storm magnet."

"What do you mean?"

"I was struck by lightning a few years ago. I lived to tell the tale, but I'm wary now."

"I can't say I blame you. That must have been a terrifying ordeal." Annabel sympathised. "I'm so glad you survived. When we have more time you must tell me all about it. You're the only person I've met who's been struck by lightning."

The toast popped up, the delicious smell drifting across the kitchen. Jaz's tummy rumbled. She jammed the phone between her chin and shoulder, listening to Annabel while putting the toast on a plate and smothering it in butter. When it came to toast, low-fat margarine didn't do it for her.

"Now, the reason I'm calling is to see if you've found the sketchbooks?"

"They were in the filing cabinet in the studio. You'll love them. You can have all but two of them for the exhibition." She bit into the toast, melted butter dripped onto her T-shirt. *Damn! I bet Annabel doesn't drop food down her front.* She rubbed at it with the corner of the tea towel not sure whether she was making it worse.

"What's in the two I can't display?"

"Me. They're full of portraits of me, as a baby, a child, a teenager, and even a couple that she must have done in the last couple of weeks before she died when I didn't know I was being observed." As she thought about her mother the all too familiar lump rose in her throat.

"Wow! Sounds amazing. Could I see them sometime? Or are they too personal?"

Jaz tried to swallow the lump, but it burst from her mouth in a spluttery cough. "Sorry, bit of toast went down the wrong way. I'd be happy to show you, but they're not to be exhibited."

"Fair enough. Ah, the other thing! The bottle. Do you have that too?"

The bottle! The one in the secret room. Jaz chewed on her lip, deciding whether to divulge its location. Much as she liked Annabel, she wasn't sure she wanted to share with her what had happened. She might react like Grandma, and Annabel was in much easier reach of the men in white coats. "No, it wasn't in the studio, but don't give up hope yet. I may be able to track it down."

"Super. Perhaps I could come and collect the sketchbooks sometime?"

"No problem."

"I'm not sure when. I'm quite busy for the next couple of days. I'll call you soon."

"Okay. Bye, Annabel."

Jaz finished her toast and licked her lips. The spectre of the bottle floated to the front of her mind. Until she'd seen it in the hidden room she'd forgotten its compelling allure. For an inanimate object it exuded an almost tangible energy that she found disturbing, but impossible to resist. Like a new lover it possessed her until she could think of nothing else.

She wondered how it had got into the secret room. The date on her mother's painting of the hands reaching for the bottle was less than eight months old. Jaz felt certain it had been painted from life not memory. If the bottle had been in her mother's studio so recently, somebody—her mother?—must have found a way into the secret room. Was there another way in? And why hide it there?

The more she thought about it, the more she wanted it.

Chapter Eight

For the most part, Jaz was sure Rick's assessment that the library had been altered to accommodate the hidden room was accurate, but a little bit of her still balked at the idea of secret places and dissolving walls. She had to check it out for herself. Just to be sure. She paced the hallway counting her strides.

"Twelve, thirteen, fourteen."

And then into the dining room, where she plastered her body along the back wall, heels to the skirting board, and repeated her pacing, until her toes reached the opposite wall.

"Almost seven. Nearly halfway."

She rushed down the hallway, and repeated her task in the library, stopping short as she reached the shelves. She estimated the depth of the shelves. "Five and half."

No doubt about it. Rick had been right. One and half strides missing.

Back in the hallway, she ascertained the location of the partitioned space and ran her hands over the surface, examining it for any trace of a concealed entry. Nothing. Not even a ripple in the wallpaper. Then again there hadn't been a ripple in the wallpaper in the attic until the storm began. She stopped dead, then glanced up at the landing, as a spark of realisation ignited.

The storm.

Whisper had leapt into the wall when the thunderclap frightened him, and at that exact moment the room had blazed with lightning. Almost instantly, the wall closed, refusing her admission...until the next lightning flash.

She rubbed her scar, wondering whether she was inextricably linked to lightning. Was that possible? Was it hunting her out? She thought about the things Ted had told her. The confluence of ley lines, the standing stones that encircled her home. Were they attracting lightning to them, or had the ancients put the stones here because of it, to mark the place? Last night the storm had centred on the house. Now she thought about it, over the course of her lifetime lots of storms had been like that. Terrifyingly close as they unleashed their fury. Sometimes she would hide under the bed, fingers in her ears waiting for the storm to wear itself out. Since Whisper moved in she tried to project an attitude of calm, even though her insides churned. Cat's picked up on distress and she didn't want to cause him any grief. A vicious storm caused enough fear without a jittery woman adding to the mix. If she communicated calm, Whisper might not freak out.

Ted maintained that lightning didn't strike in the same place twice, but he was wrong. It had hit a tree near the outbuildings when she was a child. From her bedroom window, she'd cried as the flames engulfed her swing, which had hung from the strongest branch. She'd watched her mother and a couple of the neighbours silhouetted against the raging flames as they tried to prevent the fire spreading. When, with siren blaring, the fire brigade arrived, she had hoped to see them unleash their hose, but the pelting rain had drenched everything, and so the men stood around watching the fire burn out. A few days later the decimated tree had been removed.

Jaz had been only metres from the spot when the lightning found her a decade later.

She leant her cheek on the hall wall, rubbing against it. The bottle was so close. She knew in her core that it wanted liberating, it hated being trapped in the eerie green-lit space. She had to get it out. Had to rescue it.

She wandered back into the library, and looked out of the window. Not a cloud in the sky. No chance of a repeat of last night's storm then. And if her theory was correct, no chance of the wall dissolving.

There was only one thing for it. Jaz approached the shelves, picked up as many books as she could carry and leant them against the wall beneath the window. She worked as fast as she could, trotting back and forth. The muscles in her shoulders protested as she cleared shelf after shelf, metre after metre, of her great-grandfather's precious books. As she staggered down the stepladder with the final pile she realised her task had barely begun, but she didn't care, she wanted the bottle. Had to retrieve it. The need for it burnt deep within her. It called to her. She could hear it whispering her name.

Not Jaz, not Jasmine.

Aisha.

* * *

Once bare of books, the expert craftsmanship that had been wrought to create the shelving became evident. The mellow oak gleamed as the sunlight played along the carved edges. Jaz yanked on one of the shelves, it stuck fast. She tried another. Same story. She studied the perfect dovetailed joints and realised they wouldn't be easy to rend asunder. She'd need tools. Ted had enough to open his own hardware store in one of the outhouses.

As she took the bunch of keys from the pantry the phone started to ring. She glanced at it, then down the hallway.

Aisha.

The bottle uttered her name, wanted her to ignore the insistent ringing. Nothing must distract her. Her priority was to retrieve the precious artefact. Consumed by a sense of urgency, she fumbled with the keys hurrying to unlock the backdoor. It didn't matter who was calling, only the bottle mattered. The answer phone picked up. She stepped into the garden. The sun kissed her skin and the breeze caressed her.

Grandma Faye's voice boomed from the kitchen, and Jaz stopped dead.

"Jasmine. Damn girl! Where are you?...I remembered something about the house...about the attic..."

Jaz's pulse quickened. She hurtled back into the kitchen and grabbed the phone. "Grandma, I'm here. What's that about the attic?"

"I'd completely forgotten, but you triggered something in my memory."

"What?"

Aisha.

Jaz's stomach lurched. She tried to ignore the mellifluous voice competing with Grandma Faye's harsh rasp.

"When I was a child, my aunt Alicia used to come and stay for the summer. I doubt you'll remember her. She died when you were about six years old. She brought my cousins, Peter and Elise, and we'd spend most of the time playing in the garden or down by the river..."

Get on with it, thought Jaz. Her grandma, normally so concise, was waffling.

"...One day, when I was about four or five, the weather was terrible, a massive storm. Thunder and lightning going on and on for ages."

The little hairs on the nape of Jaz's neck stood to attention.

"So we had to play indoors. We were playing hide and seek and I went up to the attic—the one your mum used as a bedroom. It was a storeroom when I was a child. I was looking for the perfect hiding place in the shadows when I tripped over something. I fell and expected to bang into the wall. At that moment, lightning lit the room..."

Jaz gasped.

"...the wall melted and I slid into it. I could feel it squeezing me and pulling me in."

Vindicated. No doubt about it. It had happened before, not only to her and Whisper. She danced from foot to foot. "What happened next?"

"Hands grabbed my ankles and I could hear my mother screaming, 'You can't have her!' and pulling me back. I thought I was going to be torn in two. I swear I grew a couple of inches! Eventually, the wall released me and mum and I fell in a heap."

"And the wall?"

"Rock solid."

"Did it happen again?"

"Not to me. My mother had locks put on the doors to keep me out. She needn't have bothered. I hated the attics, after that. I hardly ever ventured up there again, even after I forgot all about the wall trying to swallow me alive. Horrible spooky place."

"It's not horrible now. Mum made it lovely."

"I dare say she did. She had a flair for that sort of thing, even as a kid. Still, I didn't understood why she liked it up there. She had a perfectly nice room on the first floor, but she always had a mind of her own."

"I know. I remember Nanalu trying to dissuade her from moving up there, but she ignored her."

"She could always twist my mother round her little finger."

Jaz switched the receiver to her other ear. "Did Mum ever go into the wall?"

Grandma Faye sighed. "I don't know. Not that I know of, but she probably wouldn't have told me anyway. We weren't that close, you know."

Jaz sensed her grandmother's sadness. It must be horrible to lose a child, she thought, even a grown up one, even one you weren't close too.

"Didn't she say anything to you?" Grandma Faye asked.

"No, not a word." Jaz thought about the bottle. Her mother must have been into the secret room. How else did it get there?

"This morning you said the wall swallowed you?"

"That's right. Me and Whisper. We ended up in a hidden room, behind the shelves in the library." Jaz walked into the hallway, stretching the cord on the phone to its full extent. She leant out until her fingertips touched the wall.

Aisha.

"What are you going to do, Jasmine?"

Her fingertips tingled. "I don't know," she lied.

"Maybe you should leave the house. Move out."

"No!" The last thing she wanted was to leave. The house needed her. The bottle needed her.

"Well, be careful. Don't do anything silly."

"Silly? Like what?" Jaz reluctantly withdrew her fingers, straightened up and returned to the kitchen.

"I don't know. Anything dangerous."

She laughed. "That's rich coming from you. When did you ever worry about danger?"

Grandma Faye joined in her laughter. "Oh, I worried about it, but then I did it anyway. Be careful, that's all I'm saying. I don't want anything to happen to you. We've precious little family left, as it is."

Jaz hung up and pondered her grandmother's words. Without a doubt she was messing with things she didn't understand, and had little control over. Grandma Faye was right, since Mum died they only had each other. Well, there was Grandma Faye's brother Brendon, but he lived in New Zealand, and they hadn't seen him in the last decade. She'd be daft to take any unnecessary risks. She went back to the library, where precarious towers of books leant against each other trying to maintain equilibrium. If one stack tumbled the rest would follow. She should return them to the shelves. Back where they belonged. Forget about the hidden room. Forget about the bottle.

Careful not to upset the delicate balance, she picked up half a dozen weighty tomes. She couldn't remember whereabouts they were from and chose a shelf at random.

Aisha. Aisha.

Jaz screwed shut her eyes, shook her head, trying to dispel the voice. But it became more insistent, more seductive, no longer in her head, but a presence sliding around her, gossamer wisps stroking her, clothing her in a silken web, making goose pimples ripple down her arms and legs.

For several seconds she revelled in the sensation, unable to concentrate on her task. Something soft stroked her ankle, pressed against her, flickered along her calf. She opened her eyes, looked down. Whisper.

The spell broke.

The voice faded away, and a sense of being bereft seeped in, quickly washed away by relief that she was back in control. She needed to leave the library, leave the house, because she hadn't the strength to resist the bottle. If it could so easily seduce her when trapped behind the wall, what hope had she of ever again having a will of her own if she liberated it? Books clutched to her chest, she backed away from the shelves.

Aisha.

Louder. More assertive.

Goosebumps rose on her arms. The voice tore at her soul, begging for release, and her resolve slipped. Her heel caught on the edge of the rug and staggering she lost her balance and collided with the towers of books. Whisper bolted as they fell like dominoes, one after the other, covers splaying open, pages bending and creasing. Her grandfather must be spinning in his grave.

Jaz barely cared, and tossed the volumes in her arms onto the heap. The only thing that mattered was the bottle. She had to have it. They belonged together.

Chapter Nine

Jaz foraged through the tool shed. Opening a drawer filled with screwdrivers she chastised herself for not having thought of looking here before, although she no longer needed one to start her car. The letter opener sufficed and was far more attractive. She closed the drawer. A selection of chisels lay on the bench. They looked useful. She selected a couple of hefty ones and a hammer. With a bit of luck she'd be able to dismantle the shelves without too much trouble. Turning towards the open door, she noticed a thick wooden handle poking out from behind it. She swung the door back, and cheered, delighted at her find.

A sledgehammer.

Perfect. Now she could knock a hole in the wall. She dragged it out. Gasping at its weight, she lifted it, and wondered if she'd have the strength to swing it. She'd be worn out by the time she carried it to the house. She went into the garden and located the wheelbarrow, then put her chosen tools into it and trundled back to the house.

Jaz hoped to dismantle the shelves without damaging them, but found she didn't have either the skills or the patience. She prised the shelves apart using the chisels, hammer and brute force. Sweat beaded on her forehead, and she rubbed it away with her wrist, hardly pausing in her task.

Wood split, splinters flew and decorative edging chipped as shelf by shelf she demolished the library. The pile of debris grew until it rivalled the heap of books.

The activity stilled the voice. Balanced on the top of the stepladder, she forced the chisel behind the last strip of oak casing, and struck it with the hammer until the wood groaned. The plaster-coated screws gave up their hold, clattering to the floor as she wrenched the wood from the wall, and flung it on the pile.

Jaz skipped down the ladder, and stood back to admire her handiwork. Pitted and scarred, only the wall stood between her and the bottle. Her blood quickened. She hefted the sledgehammer, adjusted her grip and swung at the wall, struggling to keep her balance. A chunk of plaster crumbled. She coughed on the dust as it caught in her throat. Bare brick showed through. She balanced the sledgehammer on her shoulder, took a deep breath and let it out in a grunt as she swung again. Her arms trembled as they absorbed the reverberations. More plaster fell away. Her energy sapped with each swing of the heavy hammer, but sheer determination provided the strength to carry on.

Finally, the mortar gave and the bricks inched away. Panting, she took aim and with all her might smashed the steel hammerhead into the centre of the concave area. She jerked forward as the hammer broke through and a handful of bricks cascaded down the other side, into the secret room.

Jaz pulled the hammer back, dropped it on the floor and pressed her face to the gap. Her nose wrinkled, the bad smell from the well was stronger than she remembered. Her eyes adjusted to the eerie green light and found the bottle. The beautiful, perfect bottle. She could hardly believe she'd left it, but there had been no way to manage that and Whisper.

She tore her gaze away and focussed on her task. She used the sledgehammer to enlarge the hole, terrified that a loose brick might somehow smash into the bottle and break it. Eventually the hole was big enough for her to climb through. She kicked some bricks to the side. One fell down the well. No splash just a dull thud, and then a deep rumbling sound. Her stomach clenched. She had to rescue the bottle. Edging around the hole, not daring to look into its depths, she approached her quarry.

She bent in front of it, transfixed by its glowing, red, orange and a flicker of blue. She reached out.

A barely audible sigh. She sensed the bottle was pleased with her. She ran her hands over its smooth surface, picked it up, and hugged it to her chest.

Never again would it be locked in the dark. Never again. She clambered through the gap back into the library. She'd rescued the bottle. Her bottle.

Aisha. The sound came from the hidden room.

Chapter Ten

Jaz jumped over rubble and books and hastened from the room. The voice must be coming from the well. What the hell was down there? She closed the door, not ready to make any more discoveries. All she wanted was the bottle.

Dust and grime clung to the vessel's surface, dulling the intensity of the colours. Jaz carried it to the kitchen, set it on the draining board, and filled the sink with a gentle solution of washing up liquid and water. With the greatest care she sponged the dirt away, then dried it on a soft cloth until it gleamed.

Pleased with her efforts, she turned the bottle from side to side. The colours danced, twirling and twisting, like flames. She understood Nanalu's love of the bottle, and wondered why her great-grandfather had been prepared to give it to a stranger. Had it not had the same hold over him? Had he been sure that Nanalu would become his wife if he gave it to her, and hence it would stay in his possession? She didn't know the answers to her questions, but she knew *she* wouldn't part with it.

Intrigued by the swaying of the colours Jaz held it aloft trying to fathom the cause, but could see nothing to provide a clue about its nature. Unsure whether it employed some sort of optical illusion she tried to remove the stopper in order to view the inside. The stopper refused to budge. She ran it under water, careful not to have the temperature too hot. The last thing she wanted was to break the precious vessel. Despite her best efforts she couldn't loosen the bottle's grip on the stopper. Frustrated, she scoured the kitchen for inspiration searching for something to lubricate the join, and settled on a bottle of olive oil. She ran a ragged fingernail between the neck and stopper, then dripped two tiny drops of thick yellow oil on the rim, rubbing it in with her fingertips. All to no avail.

Finally, Jaz accepted that the stopper was fused to the neck and no amount of cajoling and teasing would separate them. The bottle would hold onto its secret as it had for centuries prior.

Her stomach rumbled, she hadn't eaten since breakfast and had drunk only two glasses of water. She glanced at the microwave clock. Past eight. No wonder she needed food. The day had disappeared. She stuffed the last two Jaffa cakes from the box into her mouth, hardly tasting them as she warmed a tin of baked beans and made more toast. She'd not the energy to make anything more elaborate. She scoffed the meal with such rapidity she knew she'd end up with indigestion, but didn't care.

Bone weary and yawning, she rubbed her aching shoulder, and stretched her muscles. Even though the sun hadn't gone down, she needed her bed. She'd be hard pressed to clean herself, let alone the dirty dishes. She left them on the worktop. They could wait until morning.

Jaz locked the back door and shot the bolt home. She caressed the bottle as she picked it up, and hugged it to her chest, deciding to return to its place it on Nanalu's display cabinet on the landing. Under the twinkling lights of the chandelier, it had always held pride of place, its ethereal beauty throwing the other bottles into shadow.

As she started to ascend the stairs she heard the clatter of the cat flap and then Whisper's miaow announcing his return and calling for her attention.

"I'm here," she called, from halfway up the flight. "I'm going for a shower and then to bed."

His bell tinkled and his claws clicked as he bounded down the tiled hallway. He hurtled up the stairs, crossing in front of her as she reached the top step. Afterwards, she couldn't be sure whether his timing was amiss, or whether her exhaustion had caused her to dodge at the wrong time. It didn't matter, the damage had been done.

She tripped over him. He disentangled himself and shot along the landing. The bottle flipped from her grasp and somersaulted through the air. Sprawled across the landing, her hand stretched out. She scrambled forward trying to catch it, but her reach was too short. It slammed into the edge of the display cabinet.

Jaz screamed. Glass flew and sprayed far and wide. A shard stabbed into the back of her hand, another lodged into her cheek, but she hardly registered the stinging pain as the colours inside the bottle leapt to life, licks of flame whirling, stretching, soaring, spinning round and round the hallway, a tornado in full force. The chandelier shook, its crystals rattled. Trembling with fear, she bum shuffled backwards and tucked herself into a corner, trying to make herself as small as possible. She held her hands over her face, watching through the gaps between her fingers. She looked towards the cabinet expecting to spot Whisper cowering there, but he hadn't taken refuge from the maelstrom. Green eyes wide, he sat in the centre of the landing, exhibiting no sign of alarm, as the inferno danced around him, not singeing his fur.

The sheet of colour shimmered, consuming the space from floor to ceiling, reaching from wall to wall. It flickered past her time after time, but never touched her. Eventually, she reached out a hand, half scared that she'd be burnt by the fairy fire. The insubstantial substance slid around her, not touching her skin. She felt nothing: no heat, no pain, no texture.

Back pressed to the wall she pushed herself to a standing position, her legs wobbled then steadied. She took a minute to control her nerves, not sure if what she was about to do was sheer madness. Taking a deep breath, she forced herself to step into the flame.

It shrank back, and she let out a breath. More confident, she took another step and then another. Each time it made way for her, ensuring no physical contact. She reached Whisper, scooped him into her arms and looked into his eyes.

"Have you any idea what's going on here?"

He purred and looked toward the cavorting flame. No longer a turbulent whirlwind, it had slowed its action to a sinuous undulation, its colour intensifying as it contracted to a cylindrical shape, less than two metres in height and a metre in diameter. It snaked along the landing and stopped before her and Whisper, the colours revolving around the transparent core.

"Oh, shit! We should have left the bottle where it was." Jaz burrowed her fingers into Whisper's fur.

"No, you shouldn't." The voice thundered around the hallway, echoing as it bounced off the walls.

Startled she jumped, spun around scanning the hallway and stairs, then leant over the balcony. "Who said that? Who's there?"

"It was I, Balmanza." The chandelier rattled, crystal droppers tinkling as the voice reverberated.

"Who? Who the hell are you? You say it like I should recognise your name. And where the hell are you?" Jaz squeezed Whisper till he squealed, and wriggled his way from her arms. Sat by her feet, he poked his head through the banister rails.

"Right here." The flame moved in front of them, hovering twelve feet above the tiled hall floor.

Jaz's stomach clenched. "Oh my God! You? You talk? What on earth are you?"

"You would call me a genie."

"Shit! You've got to be kidding! They only exist in fairy tales. Any chance you could turn the volume down? My hearing's quite good, you're going to deafen me."

"My humble apologies. I am adjusting." Balmanza's voice dropped to a normal speaking volume.

"Thank you." She caught the back of her hand on the banister and winced. The shard of glass still protruded. Gently she removed it. Blood trickled, she sucked at it, but when she removed it from her mouth the blood showed no sign of stopping. An arm of flame flickered across her hand, and then pulled back. Jaz blinked and rubbed her eyes. The blood had vanished along with the cut. "How? How did you do that?"

"I'm a genie." The flame spiralled and turned bright orange.

"Straight up? You're a genie in a bottle?"

"No longer trapped in a bottle." It raced around the hallway, skimming the walls and ceiling. "I have waited so long to be released. Waited for my new master to set me free."

"Me?" Jaz shook her head. How cool was that? She had her own genie. "Strictly speaking I'd be your mistress."

Balmanza stopped in front of her. "Not you."

"What do you mean, not me? I'm the one who got you out of the secret room, I'm the one who did all the work and I'm the one who dropped you."

"You wouldn't have dropped me if my master hadn't tripped you."

"Your master?" She looked at Whisper. He licked a paw and stroked it through his whiskers. "You mean Whisper? Whisper my cat."

"Not any cat. Whisper of Lightning."

Chapter Eleven

Incandescent light flickered forming shadows on the walls and ceiling as Balmanza hovered over the staircase.

Bewildered, Jaz sat down on the top step, and stared at her cat.

"Unbelievable," she muttered. "Whisper. My Whisper, the stray I adopted, is the master of a real life genie."

Balmanza came close and whispered, "What if it was Whisper who did the adopting not you?"

Jaz raised an eyebrow, she'd not thought of it like that before. She bit the sharp end of her thumbnail trying to tidy it.

"It's still not fair," she said. "I did all the hard work, destroying the library, swinging the sledgehammer, clearing rubble, not to mention ruining what's left of my nails in the process. What use can a cat make of a genie? Some extra fish or slower mice to chase? Much as I love Whisper I can't see him making the best use of his newfound power. It will be wasted on him."

"That's his prerogative."

She beckoned Whisper to her. He trotted over and settled onto her lap. She looked into his inscrutable face and wondered what went on in his little head. More than she'd ever guessed, she realised.

She returned her focus to Balmanza. "So does Whisper have three wishes?" she asked.

"He has as many as he wants. I am his to command for the rest of his life."

"One of them or all nine?" she asked sarcastically.

Balmanza said something in a language she didn't understand, but she got the distinct impression she hadn't furthered her case. He bent in front of Whisper, and made a sound almost like a deep purring. Whisper responded by stretching out his paw and extending his claws. Balmanza dipped down, and then raced around the chandelier several times before coming to a rearing halt before them. If he'd been a car there'd be the smell of burning rubber.

Jaz looked with astonishment from one to the other. Had Whisper told the genie what to do, or was Balmanza showing off? She'd no idea what was going on between the two of them. She shook her head. What was she doing, sitting on the stairs talking to a genie who looked like a ball of flaming gas? Maybe he wasn't the only one flaming. She must be flaming mad to believe this was real. Part of her thought she might be dreaming. Perhaps she'd been knocked unconscious when she tripped, but she couldn't remember banging her head. *Oh well, in for a penny.* "What about me? Don't I get any wishes?"

"No."

"Not even a teeny-weeny one?" She thought about her battered car. "A new convertible Mini would be nice. That wouldn't be too much to ask, would it? After all, without me you'd be trapped for all eternity."

Balmanza reared upwards, stretching till he reached the ceiling, his voice thundered. "Weren't you listening? Whisper of Lightning is my master. Only he can command me. You get nothing. Nothing. Do you understand?"

She shrank back, quaking beneath his wrath. Maybe he'd turn her into a toad. Well, see if she cared, he didn't have a monopoly on anger; her temper was rising like bread dough on a summer day. She tipped her head backwards and looked up the length of the flickering red flame. "Okay, you don't have to shout. I get it. I receive nothing for my efforts. Not one piddling little wish. Whisper of Lightning gets the lot."

"At last, you understand."

Was he doing a jig? Pompous ass! She hoped he wasn't going to become a pain in the neck. Since he belonged to Whisper and Whisper lived with her, she had a feeling they'd be seeing a lot of each other from now on. She took a deep breath and decided to try being less aggressive. "Why do you call him Whisper of Lightning?"

Balmanza swirled into a loop then shrank until he was under two metres tall. "It is his name."

"Whisper's his name. I know that. I gave it to him. It's the *of Lightning* bit I don't understand. What's that about?"

"You are Lightning. He is yours, you are his. He is Whisper of Lightning. You are Lightning of Whisper."

Whisper purred and rubbed the top of his head against her wrist. She stroked his ears.

She wagged a finger at Balmanza. "No, no, no. You've got this wrong. I'm Jaz, Jasmine if you prefer. And if I'm dancing I'm Aisha. You know that because that's the name you used when you were calling me to rescue you. Note you were calling for me, not Whisper."

"Yes, you have many names, but I didn't use any. Someone else is calling you."

A shiver ran down her spine. "Who?"

"You'll find out when the time is right."

"Why not now?"

"The time isn't right."

Jaz rolled her eyes. "Do you have to be so obtuse?"

Balmaza didn't answer.

"Nobody has ever called me Lightning," she said.

"But that is who you are."

Suddenly unnerved she trembled, and her scar tissue tingled. She rubbed her shoulder. "Because of the lightning strike?"

He turned around, and his centre glowed deep blue. As he completed a revolution the blue moved out towards the edge of his form consuming all of the red colour. "You were destined to be struck so that Whisper could find you. It was predicted."

Destiny? Predictions? This was crazy. "Who predicted it? Why?"

"When my last master trapped me in the bottle, he said I'd be trapped there until the Whisper of Lightning released me. I've been imprisoned for millennia, waiting to travel to this place, waiting for today." He flitted around the room again, like a giant firefly, changing colours with such rapidity that they merged into a blur.

Jaz pressed her fingers to her temples. "Can you please stop that twirling? You're like a whirling dervish. You're making me dizzy."

He stopped a few feet from her and swayed lazily from side to side. The movement entranced her, and her eyelids sagged. Her head buzzed trying to make sense of everything. She rubbed her eyes and yawned, hoping the oxygen would revive her. Her anger had dissipated, exhaustion returned, dragging at her muscles and fogging her brain. "Why didn't Whisper release you before?"

"He tried. He knocked the bottle from the table in the painting studio. The Mother of Lightning had reflexes to match her name. She managed to catch it and my imprisonment continued. Fortunately for me, your reflexes don't match hers."

Her eyes opened wide. "Mum? You mean Mum, my mum caught you?"

"Yes, aren't you listening? Theresa."

Her mother saved the bottle. "When?"

"On midwinter day."

"Back in December? Six months ago." Suddenly a thought occurred to her. "Wait a minute, today is midsummer's day. Is that significant?"

"Of course. There are only two days a year when I could be released. Midwinter and midsummer."

Jaz ran her hand across her forehead, pressed her fingers where a headache threatened. "How did you get into the secret room?"

"The Mother of Lightning put me there to stop Whisper breaking the bottle and liberating me."

"She didn't mention it to me. Did she know you were in there?"

"How could she?"

"I don't know." Her eyelids drooped. Forcing them open she tried to shake off drowsiness. "I don't appear to know much of anything anymore.

Balmanza swayed from side to side, his voice took on the soothing tones of a lullaby. "Lightning. You have done well. Now you must sleep."

"What about you? What will you do?"

"I've been imprisoned for centuries long. I have much to do, but I will return whenever Whisper of Lightning calls me."

Whisper jumped from her lap and ran down the stairs and across the hallway. Balmanza shrank to the size of a tennis ball, hovered to the left of Whisper's head and accompanied him. They disappeared from view as they went into the kitchen.

Jaz glanced around the hall. A bit dusty from all the demolition work she'd done, and quite ordinary without Balmanza bathing it all in his radiance. She got to her feet, turned towards her bedroom and picked her way through the broken glass sprinkled on the carpet. Without the extraordinary contents the fragments appeared commonplace, the same as regular glass despite their undoubted age.

"I should have got the genie to clear that up!" she muttered.

Chapter Twelve

Not stirring until the sound of Ted cutting the beech hedge awakened her, Jaz awoke fully clothed. She stretched and groaned at the ache in her shoulders and back. Memories of the previous evening flooded her consciousness, and she jumped from the bed and rushed to the landing.

No sign of Whisper or the genie, but the broken glass lay where she had left it, twinkling in the sunlight. She'd better clear it up before she or Whisper stood on a piece. She made her way downstairs to fetch a dustpan and brush and the vacuum cleaner. As she reached the hallway, her stomach heaved and she clamped a hand over her nose and mouth.

"Oh, my God! What is that smell?" The putrid stench of something rotting, something foul made her pores want to close. Instinctively she knew the source. Her hand trembled as she opened the library door a mere few inches, afraid of what she'd find. The smell grew stronger and she gagged, then she peered through the gap and cringed at the sight before her. What had possessed her? She'd wrecked the room, her favourite room.

Jaz pushed the door open to its full extent and entered the library. She raced through the heaps of books to the windows, and flung them open, gasping lungful after lungful of fresh summer air.

She turned her gaze back to the room, hardly able to comprehend that she had single-handedly wrought such destruction. Maybe she should join a demolition crew; it looked like she had a talent for wrecking. She sucked in more fresh air, held her breath and climbed over the books and rubble into the secret room. She fought to hold her breath as the bad smell emanating from the well became stronger. She peered into its glowing green depths. Her lungs burned and she became dizzy. Unable to hold on any longer, the breath shot from her body and she breathed in the stench. She doubled over, retched and a stream of bile poured from her mouth and down the well. A deep noise rumbled from the depths. She jumped backwards, wiped her mouth with the back of her hand and edged away, her gaze fixed on the rim of the pit.

Relieved to reach the hallway, Jaz closed the door wishing there was a lock. She went to the kitchen and turned on the tap. Using her hand to cup water she rinsed her mouth, and spat bile into the stream running down the drain.

The hairs on the back of her neck stirred. Certain she was being watched she spun around, scanning the room. Nobody there. Not even Whisper. She wondered where he had gone and whether he'd come back now he had a new friend. Chiding herself for being nervous, she turned on the radio.

She picked up the phone and dialled Rick's number, already memorised. "Hi, it's Jaz."

"Nice to hear from you."

She loved the way the timbre of his voice changed when he realised who was calling.

"What can I do for you?" he asked.

Ooh, don't tempt me. No. Don't flirt. This is business. "You remember that hidden room you thought there might be in my library?"

"Yes. Are you planning to open it?" His voice lost the seductive tone, turning professional.

"Possibly." No point trying to explain over the phone what she'd done, let him see the damage for himself. "I'd like you to give me some advice about it."

"Okay. Have you looked to see if there's a secret door or sliding panel?"

"Err...no. That hadn't occurred to me." Good grief! What if she'd wrecked the library and there was an easy way in! No subtlety; that was her problem.

"I could pop round. Say about seven."

"Sorry, I'm dancing tonight. Can you come earlier?"

"Afraid not. Best I can do is tomorrow morning about eight-thirty."

"Okay. See you then."

Jaz hung up. Damn! She'd have to live with this awful whiff for another day at least. She rooted in the cupboard under the sink and found a can of air freshener, shook it, then holding it aloft, walked through the hallway spraying it in front of her. She opened the library door just enough to squeeze the nozzle through and gave it a good long blast of honeysuckle scent.

She closed the door, and put the can on the hallstand. She'd a feeling she'd be needing it a lot over the next day or two. She took a pile of rags from the hall cupboard and stuffed them into the gap at the bottom of the library door. Anything to help keep the smell at bay.

She caught a glimpse of herself in the mirror. Scary. After sleeping for twelve hours straight in yesterday's dirty clothes and still caked in grime she could have passed for a tramp. Another transformation would be required before going to her dance class tonight. She glanced at the clock. She must check through her crossword puzzle and put in the last couple of clues, she had a deadline to meet.

She ran upstairs to shower, realised she still hadn't cleared the glass and trotted back down for the dustpan. Back on the landing she scooped the bits into a pile. She held one of the larger pieces up to the light, it had lost all its allure. Nothing special. Balmanza's trapped energy had provided the colour and mystery she associated with the beautiful bottle. However intrigued she'd been by it, never in her wildest dreams had she thought a genie resided there. She dropped the fragments into the wastepaper bin in her bedroom and headed to the bathroom.

Chapter Thirteen

An Alabina CD filled the Mini with music as Jaz headed home. Dance class had been a hoot, and she congratulated herself on finally mastering a tricky combination of layered undulations and spin turns. She loved going to class and laughing and joking with the other women, especially timid Alice whose shyness disappeared the minute a spotlight turned on her, and Claire who constantly fought against her natural lack of grace but danced with such pleasure it was impossible not to enjoy her peformances.

As she turned right at the roundabout she noticed the road she'd driven down plunge into darkness.

"Here we go again," she spoke out loud.

This hadn't happened for a few months now. Ever since being hit by lightning she'd had a strange relationship with electricity. For weeks at a time nothing would happen, then she'd notice streetlights turning off as she drove by, and small electrical appliances frying their circuits. So far four kettles had died on her, six toasters and she'd lost count of how many hairdryers she'd replaced. After her second ipod succumbed she gave up using personal music players.

Out of habit, Jaz turned onto the country road instead of taking the bypass. Clouds had rolled in, obliterating the moon and stars. She switched to full beam, and approached the stretch of road works with care. Lanterns hung from barriers highlighting the danger. The road surface had been torn up and the Mini juddered over the loose stones at snail's pace. Halfway along, she heard the rhythmic thwop, thwop, thwop of a flat tyre.

"No! Please, God, no."

She stopped the car. The only other vehicles in sight were massive diggers and steamrollers parked up for the night. She climbed out and saw the rear tyre on the driver's side was well and truly flat.

"Shit! Shit! Shit!" Jaz kicked the defunct tyre. "Not fair! Not funny. Not dressed like this." She looked down at her sequined bra and the layered chiffon skirts. "Why? Why now?"

Under the accumulated detritus in the boot, Jaz located the jack and wheel brace, and cursing the dusty road, bent to the task of changing the wheel. Skirts fluttering in the breeze, she fitted the jack into position and loosened the first nut with ease, but the next one refused to budge no matter how much force she applied. She rubbed a film of sweat from her forehead, and then stood up, put her foot on the tyre iron and, grunting with effort, pushed with all her might. The nut refused to move.

She screamed in frustration, and banged her fist on the roof of the car. A sudden blast of wind whipped her skirts into a frenzy of fabric that covered her face. She batted it down with her hands, plastering it in clumps at hip level. Her skin crawled. She could feel eyes burrowing into her back, but when she spun around certain someone would be standing there, she couldn't see a soul. The hedgerow rustled and her blood froze. Back pressed along the side of the car, she scanned the area and eased her way to the driver's door. With shaking hands she fumbled with the handle, finally managed to open it and scooted into the car, locking the door behind her.

She closed the windows, glancing up and down the road. Nothing. No headlamps in either direction. She could be stuck here till morning. She flicked on the overhead light and pulled her cell phone from her bag. The protective rubber cover helped the device survive the electrical surges she transmitted. She fumbled with the buttons and let out a sigh of relief when she saw the transmission signal. She dialled Ted's number. When he answered, she could hear voices in the background and a peel of laughter.

"Hello, Ted. It's Jaz. I've got a flat tyre."

Ted laughed. "Well, you know what to do. I taught you that when you got your licence."

"I know, I tried, but I can't loosen the bloody nuts."

"Where are you?"

"On the old road, about two miles past Harper's Corner. There's some road works. I'm there." A shadow fell across her. "Aargh!" She scuttled away from the door and looked in its direction, but once again she could identify nothing out of place.

"Jaz, are you all right?"

"I'm jumping at shadows, but please come quick, Ted. It's really spooky out here."

She hung up, but held onto her phone as she scrutinised the landscape. She looked around for a weapon, checked her bag, then knelt on the seat, leaning across the backseat and pawing through the accumulated CD cases, magazines, some dirty sports gear and handful of cosmetics. Her hand closed on the handle of a hairbrush.

"Surely there's something better than this!"

Jaz tossed it back onto the rear seat. As she slumped back onto her seat, she spotted the bejewelled letter opener glinting in the ignition. She pulled it out and held it up to the light. It looked pretty pathetic and she'd have to be Within a few feet of an assailant to be able to use it, but it was the best she could do. She wished she'd been practising a sword dance tonight. She held the tiny dagger point outwards in front of her chest. Desperate for Ted's headlights to come down the road, she estimated how long it would take.

Two minutes to get in the car.

Three minutes to get out of Fletcher's Cross.

Maybe another five to Harper's Corner.

Then three more to reach her.

Thirteen minutes.

She sighed. Thirteen minutes and he'd be here. She could cope for thirteen minutes. He'd be picking up his keys, getting in...

Something thudded on the roof. Jaz screamed and curled into a ball. The car shook. She trembled, turned and tried to squeeze under the steering wheel, but couldn't fit. The Mini rattled as the vibrations increased, the glove box dropped open, the contents spilling out, rolling onto the floor and under the seat. She covered her head with her hands and closed her eyes.

Was this how she was going to die? Where the hell was Ted? He should be here by now.

The car shook more violently. She lifted her head and peered through the windows. Dark shapes whirled and twisted but she couldn't identify them. Jaz heard a sharp crack, and saw a fine split travel up the rear window, forking in several directions. One of the shapes pressed on the glass, and she feared it would give way.

"Aish...sh...sh...a. Aish...sh...sh...a."

The sound grated on her ears. Was it the wind or were the shadows calling her? She clutched the edge of the seat. When she screamed no sound came from her throat. No sound, not even a whisper.

And then, as suddenly as it started, the rattling stopped. The shapes vanished. Bright light washed through the windows, and Jaz heard the crunch of tyres and the rumble of an engine. She scrambled onto the seat, expecting to see Ted's car.

Not a car.

Not Ted.

A van.

Rick's van. Rick.

He stopped and got out. She flicked the lock, flung open the door, and hurtled into his arms.

"Wow! That's what I call a welcome," he said, embracing her. "Hey, you're shaking, are you okay?"

"I was...there was...did you see..?" Heart racing, she looked over one shoulder and then the other. The scary creatures had disappeared leaving the air calm and peaceful, the only sound the long grass sighing in the breeze. The only sign of anything untoward was the cracked window. What could she say to him that wouldn't sound crazy? "I'm fine." Reluctantly, she extracted herself from his hold. "Just spooked out here on my own. That's all."

Rick looked her up and down. "If you'd taken the bypass you'd have had plenty of knights in shining armour."

She wrapped her arms around her midriff, suddenly conscious of her attire. "Dance class. Too hot for my coat. Where's Ted? Why are you here? Not that I'm not pleased to see you or anything."

"We were in the pub. Darts night. I'd finished but Ted's playing in the last game so I said I'd come to the rescue. You okay with that?"

"Yes." More than okay. Without even knowing, he'd frightened off the scary things, but she wondered if they were still lurking, waiting for another chance to strike.

"Right, let's sort this tyre." Rick set to work.

Still jittery, Jaz kept watch on the hedgerows and fields in case the dark shapes reappeared. The stubborn nut didn't create a problem for Rick and in a matter of minutes he'd fitted the spare tyre.

He closed the boot and wiped one palm against the other. "Get in and start her up."

Jaz slid into the driver's seat, and realised the letter opener was no longer in the ignition. That's right, she'd taken it out. She must have dropped it when Rick arrived. She got out of the car again and looked around the ground.

"What are you doing?" he asked.

"Looking for something. I must have dropped it when I got out." She spotted it glinting in the light from Rick's headlamps.

She picked it up, dusted it off and slipped back into the car.

"What's that?" asked Rick.

"A letter opener. I use it to start the car."

"Normal people use keys."

Jaz managed to smile. "Who said I'm normal?"

She started the Mini first time.

"I'll follow you home if you like," he said.

"I'd appreciate that."

She waited until he turned the van around and set off, relieved to be leaving the scary place behind.

Chapter Fourteen

Gravel spat as Jaz slid the Mini into its parking space. She sat in the car, letting her breathing steady and waited for Rick to follow her onto the drive. When he alighted, she got out and joined him on the path to the front door.

"Talk about a bat out of hell," he said.

"What do you mean?"

"It took me over twelve minutes to get to you, and I was flooring it. We made it back in slightly over ten." He rubbed his hand through his hair. "Your Mini looks clapped out, but it goes like a rocket."

Jaz pulled her door key from her bag, and was about to insert it in the lock when he put his hand on her wrist, stopping her. Her heart skipped a beat. She turned, her gaze darting from side to side. Were the creepy things back? Had they followed her? "What's wrong?"

He pointed to the library windows. "They're open."

She sighed with relief. "Is that all? I must have forgotten to close them."

"You might have had burglars."

"Don't say that! That's all I need after the night I've had." She didn't believe anybody had broken in, the flowerbeds weren't trampled and the windows were exactly as she'd left them.

"Let me go in first." He held out his hand for the key.

Jaz wasn't used to being told what to do. "Listen, macho man. I've lived on my own long enough. I can go in alone."

Rick gestured towards the door and stepped away making room for her to pass. "I'm sure you can. See you." He started back down the path.

"Wait. I'm sorry."

He stopped and turned.

She shuffled from foot to foot, and bit her lip. "I'm not used to people trying to look after me."

He walked towards her and stroked her arm. "Maybe it's time you started getting used to it."

"Maybe it is," she said. She looked at the door key, and then handed it to him. "Lead the way, brave knight."

He opened the door, ran his hand along the wall and flicked on the light. She followed him in, saw nothing out of place.

"See, it's fine," she said.

"Let me check the library."

He opened the door a few inches and looked through the gap. "Bloody hell, it's been ransacked."

Jaz grabbed the can of air freshener and spraying liberally pushed past him. "I'm afraid that was me."

Eyes wide, looking from one pile of books to the next, Rick stepped into the room. "What the hell? You mean you created this havoc?" He choked on the thick chemical spray.

"Uh uh." She switched on the light, and pointed to the hole in the wall.

"Good grief! You don't do things by halves, do you?" He strode over the books and dismantled shelves and ran his hand along the rough edge of the wall where she had broken through.

"I wanted to see the secret room."

"Well, that's obvious." He shook his head, and screwed up his nose. "Euuch! What is that smell?"

He clamped a hand over his nose, and Jaz leant past him into the space and sprayed more air freshener.

"It's coming from in there. It stinks. That's why I left the windows open."

"Well that smell would sure act as a burglar deterrent."

Jaz climbed into the space, careful not to snag her layered skirts on the rubble.

He coughed and spluttered, then followed her.

"Be careful where you stand, the edge is crumbly." She pointed at the hole in the ground. "According to Ted's mother-in-law it's an old well. Can you see that strange green light that's coming out of it?"

He looked into its depths. "Some sort of phosphorescence. How deep is it?"

"I don't know. It looks misty, like something's bubbling at the bottom."

He picked up a lump of mortar and tossed it into the pit before she could stop him. A deep rumbling noise rose from the well masking the sound of the mortar hitting the bottom. He took a step back. "Wow. Did you hear that?"

"Uh yeah. It gives me the creeps. Any idea what's making it?"

"Probably a troll," he laughed.

"Very funny! I don't for a minute believe a troll resides down there. In case you don't know, Trolls only exist in fairy tales." Jaz flounced back across the debris as quickly as her full skirts would allow. "I was looking for a more scientific explanation—something to do with acoustics or the like."

She stopped by the door. Rick hadn't moved.

"Come on," she said, clutching the door handle.

He bent down and picked up a broken brick.

"No," she shouted. "Don't. Come out now, Rick. Don't throw anything else down there."

"I was joking about the troll."

"I know. But leave it alone now. You can look at it properly tomorrow when the light's better, maybe we could drop a camera down there or something."

He stood on the edge for a moment longer, before dropping the brick onto the rubble pile and walking away. "So what are you putting your money on, if you don't believe my troll theory?"

"I've no idea, but I sure don't want to drink the water if there is any. Let's have some wine," she said, wanting something to steady her nerves, still skittish from her experience with the scary things that attacked the Mini. "It's the least I can do to thank you for coming to my rescue. Then you can tell me the best way of sorting that mess out."

He pulled a face and pointed over his shoulder at the library. "You expect me to sort that out? I hope you've got a big budget."

"I'm working on it." She led the way into the living room. "Make yourself at home. Is wine okay, or something stronger?"

"Whatever you're having."

When she returned with two large glasses of merlot, Rick had put some music on the CD player, kicked off his shoes, and was sat on the sofa leaning backwards against the soft cushions. He obviously had no problem making himself at home. She handed him a glass and put hers on a side table.

"Is this something you dance to?" he asked, taking a slug of wine.

"Sometimes. I won't be a minute. I'm going to get changed into something less fancy."

"Don't," he said.

"Pardon?"

"Stay like that." He cocked his head on one side and looked her up and down. "Dance for me."

She laughed. "People pay to watch me perform."

"And people pay for my services. I'll write you an invoice. One belly dance for my super-hero rescue service." He raised an eyebrow and smiled. "Deal?"

Jaz picked up her wine, took a mouthful, watching him over the rim of her glass. She knew where this was going. If she danced for him, one thing would lead to another and before she knew it they'd be all over each other. Was that what she really wanted?

Who was she trying to kid? She'd been smitten with him since the second they met, and spent far too much of her time fantasising about him. "Okay. You've got yourself a deal, but I should apprise you of the rules."

"You've got to be kidding," he spluttered. "Rules?"

"Well, more like rule." She turned sideways on and did a sinuous belly roll. His eyes widened. "But if you're not interested..."

She headed towards the door.

"Oh, I'm interested. Definitely interested." He finished his wine.

"Let me get you some more wine, then I'll tell you."

He groaned. "You're teasing me."

"You reckon?" She shimmied her hips as she left the room, giggling to herself.

In the kitchen, Jaz loaded a tray with some cheese and crackers and half a box of Turkish delight that she only ate on special occasions. The bottle of Australian merlot was already less than half full. She took another one off the wine rack. She'd a feeling one bottle wouldn't be enough.

Back in the living room, she unscrewed the open bottle and topped up their glasses.

"So, the rule?" Rick perched on the edge of the sofa, cut off a chunk of cheese and bit into it.

She opened a drawer and pulled out her favourite coin belt, tying it around her hips. "The rule is..." She paused for effect. "No touching the belly dancer."

"You're joking."

The coins jingled as she walked across the room. From a shelf she picked up her sword, swiftly pulled it from its scabbard, and pointed it at his throat. The blade gleamed in the lamplight. "No, deadly serious," she said, her face deadpan.

He looked down the length of the blade, leaned away, not looking quite so sure of himself all of a sudden.

Jaz erupted into laughter. "Don't worry, it's a prop, but it could probably do some damage if I hit you with it. It's quite heavy."

She handed Rick the sword. He tested the weight, stood up, and swung it around, feinted a few times.

"Typical," she said, taking it from him. "You blokes always want a battle."

"It's what it's for."

"Not this one," she said. She balanced it on one shoulder, stretched her arms out and spun around half a dozen times. The sword barely wobbled. She grabbed the hilt as she stopped, and bent into a low bow.

"Impressive."

"It's my party piece." She sheathed the sword, drank some wine and picked up the remote control to select a track. "Sit down, and don't forget the rule."

When the music for her new solo filled the room Jaz lifted her arms and danced.

At the start, she felt awkward, a little embarrassed in the intimate setting of her living room, but gradually she relaxed into the music and began to enjoy herself. When Rick demanded an encore, she threw herself into a three and half minute drum solo with gusto, pleased he was so obviously enjoying her efforts. Her heart raced and she glistened with sweat as she performed the final spin and posed. She stayed on the spot, lifting her hair and catching her breath, knowing she looked alluring. He stood and walked towards her, his face solemn. His eyes, dark with desire, locked with hers. Entranced, her feet rooted to the spot. She couldn't decide whether she wanted him to make a move now or not. Whilst she found him attractive in a knees turning to jelly way, she wasn't a one-night stand type of girl, and she wasn't sure he was looking for anything longer.

Before she could say anything, he reached out, ran his index finger along her clavicle, and trailed it down her cleavage. She gasped as an erotic charge whizzed through her. He withdrew his finger, and slowly brought it to his mouth and licked her sweat from it. Her stomach flipped. It took all she had to back away from him.

"I thought you understood the rule," Jaz chided, as she picked up her wine and drained the glass.

Frown lines creased his forehead. "Something must have been lost in translation."

He sat on the edge of the settee, picked up a shoe and began to put it on. "I'll go if you like."

"No! Please don't. I'd like you to stay, it's... I don't want to rush things. I'm not trying to be a tease. I like you, but I'd like to get to know you better first." Sweating more now than when she'd stopped dancing, she stopped herself from babbling on and busied herself filling her wine glass, hoping she hadn't blown her chance. She gulped at the wine, and stole a glance at him over the rim.

"What do you want to know?" His eyes crinkled, and he dropped his shoe.

She noticed a hole in the heel of his sock. "Everything, absolutely everything."

Rick slouched back onto the settee. "That shouldn't take too long." He scratched his chin. "I've got an older sister and a younger brother..."

As he started to talk, Jaz sat on the floor, her chiffon skirts pooling around her. She leant her lower arm on the coffee table, and twiddled the stem of her wine glass, watching his lips form the words, his face animated, and his hands moving as he illustrated his story in mid-air. She wondered if he had Italian genes. It didn't take long before they relaxed into each other's company again, laughing and joking as they shared childhood antics.

Time raced by and the second bottle of wine emptied. Jaz yawned and stretched. She'd drunk more than she intended, and her tongue stumbled and slurred some of her words. Maybe she should make some coffee.

"Do you want..." A banging and rattling in the hallway stopped her mid sentence. "What the...?"

Whisper and Balmanza. It had to be. What the hell were they doing? She didn't know how she'd explain Balmanza to Rick. Oh well, he could work it out for himself, like she'd had to.

Jaz got to her feet, staggered, righted herself and went to the door. Rick followed. She opened the door and was knocked off balance. Not Balmanza. One of the scary black shapes from out on the road.

Jaz screamed.

Rick grabbed hold of her, pushed her behind him, and thrust his shoulder to the solid door, trying to close it.

She backed across the room. Scooted into the corner and cowered.

They'd found her.

Followed her home.

What the hell did they want?

What had she ever done to them?

Her pulse raced, adrenaline shooting through her, sobering her up. She willed Rick to close the door, but as his feet lost purchase, and the opening got bigger, she knew he was losing the battle.

"Aishhhhha."

Her blood turned cold as her dance name hissed through the air. They were coming for her. Rick cursed, stumbled backwards, tripped over the rug and landed flat on his back.

The shape followed, floating on air. Then another and another. Each amorphous being, like a gigantic black leaf, twisted and turned, causing the room to vibrate. Pictures on the walls flapped on their hooks, the furniture shook, ornaments fell over, the wine glasses tumbled to the floor. The first creature skimmed over Rick and came towards her. The other two engulfed him. Immobile with fear, she watched him wrestling with them.

She would be next.

Frantic, Jaz looked for a weapon. Her eyes alighted on her sword. She had to take action, she sprang to her feet and grabbed the hilt, pulling the sword from the scabbard as she dodged the leading leaf creature. It lunged at her. She thrust at it. The unsharpened blade could do little damage, but it was all she had.

She slashed the blade from side to side, trying to get past the leaf creature, to get to the door, out of the room. She stole a glance at Rick. He'd stopped moving. She ducked and swerved as the creature tried to curl around her. She poked it with the sword. Finally made contact, but the rebated edge proved ineffective. A mighty force juddered up the blade and along her arm flinging her into the air. Her muscles spasmed and she fell to the ground like a rag doll.

Winded, she lay on her back, tried to move.

Couldn't.

The leaf creature hovered over her. Hissed her name, and dropped onto her. The world went black.

Chapter Fifteen

Jaz's head throbbed. Her hip hurt and a sharp pain shot down her leg. She adjusted her position, but there was no give in the hard surface on which she lay. Her eyelids flickered.

Green.

She rubbed the back of her hand across her eyelids and then squinted at her green tinged wrist. Her eyes opened fully and she held her arms and hands out for inspection, scanning them. Definitely green. She rubbed her hands together, spat on one and rubbed again, but it stayed the same sickly shade.

The events of last night flooded back. The last thing she remembered was being swamped by the vile smelling creature. She'd fought with all her might, but had blacked out.

Sitting up, she examined her chest, her belly and her feet with growing dismay.

"Aaargh." Every bit of her was green. The creatures had turned her skin into something resembling a lizard. She choked on a tear. What else had they done to her?

She drew her knees to her chin and hugged them. How ridiculous to be wearing a belly dance costume at a time like this; all sequins and bling instead of a sensible pair of jeans and T-shirt. She took hold of the hem of the top layer of the skirt and tucked it under her bra, then she saw the dull dark splotch of a bloodstain on the lower layer. She examined herself, couldn't see any cuts. Someone else's blood? Oh God! Rick! Where was he? What had happened to him? She looked around. No Rick.

She was in a small circular room, its diameter hardly longer than her height. No furniture. The floor and walls were made of smooth, green material, same as the floor. She tapped it with her nails, recognising the brittle chinking sound.

Glass.

A glass room. They'd kidnapped her, taken her away and imprisoned her. Panic rose inside her, as heart racing her breathing became high and shallow. The room sparkled through the kaleidoscope created by unbidden tears. She dashed them away with the back of her hand and looked at her skin again, breathing a sigh of relief as she realized that the green tone was due to the cast of light filtering through some sections of the glass walls. She examined her prison. No door. No window.

"How the hell did they get me in here?" Her voice bounced back at her echoing off the smooth surface.

She looked up where the walls curved and joined the ceiling, also made of glass. In the centre a chimney disappeared into darkness.

Jaz pushed herself to her feet and walked around the perimeter of her prison, running her hands over the vertical faces in case she could find a concealed door. She jumped upwards, stretching her hands high into the air, but couldn't reach the lofty ceiling, not that there was anything to grab hold of up there. Regardless, she tried again and again. Only the chimney offered a way in or out. Exhausted and panting she slumped to the ground, well and truly trapped.

She screamed in frustration, and hammered her fists on the floor. Gradually, her screaming subsided, first into a whimper and then silence.

Jaz pressed her face against the cool glass and tried to see outside. Giant objects loomed, their edges blurred by the thick glass, colours distorted. It took her a minute to focus.

Gradually she recognised the trappings of her living room, but on an enormous scale.

"What the hell is going on? It's all massive." An inkling of comprehension stirred in her mind. Shaking her head, she stepped backwards into the centre of her glass chamber, her heart racing and blood pumping as though she'd completed a gruelling dance session. On opposite sides of the glass two rectangular sections were darker than the rest, no light passed through them. One slightly smaller than the other, neither reached the ground. She lifted the folds of her skirt and examined the bloodstain, sniffed at it, and recognised the smell. Not blood. Red wine.

Her gaze flew around her prison, as she realised where she was. Gripped with fear she turned back to the wall, and pounded on it screaming, "Let me out. Let me out."

Only silence greeted her plea. Somehow the creatures had shrunk her, and imprisoned her in a wine bottle - the patches of darkness were created by the labels. She had to get out. But how? She'd tried already without success. The only opening was the bottle neck and she couldn't reach that.

Through the glass she spotted the other empty bottle. In the bottom she could make out a dark blob. It had to be Rick.

"Rick, wake up!" Her echoing voice ricocheted around, loud and penetrating. "Wake up. We're trapped."

Rick didn't stir.

She had to escape, but then what? By her reckoning she was less than ten centimetres tall. She wondered whether she'd ended up like the Borrowers, living behind the skirting boards, and sneaking around the house, hoping nobody would see her. At least she'd be free. She shook the thought away. She'd worry about size later. First she had to find a way out.

She returned her attention to the room outside. The bottles stood side by side on the edge of the coffee table. Stretching out from under the edge of the table, she spotted a wide silver road, and realised it was her sword. It had been precious little use as a weapon last night, but now it might redeem itself.

Jaz weighed her options, mulling over her one way to escape, before accepting she had to try, regardless of the danger.

She took careful note of the sword's position, went to the opposite side of the bottle, and then ran as fast as she could, her shoulder colliding with the wall. The jarring impact hurt, but she cheered as the bottle wobbled.

It stopped.

She needed more momentum. Over and over she repeated the motion, fast enough to prevent the bottle from coming to a complete halt. Each time it tilted a little more. Her tiring muscles quivered, and her head spun dizzily, her sense of balance challenged by the swaying motion. Once more she ran at the side and her stomach lurched as the bottle reached tipping point. She pushed her weight on and off the side, hoping her weight shifts would tip the balance. The next second, the bottle tumbled heading for the sword. There was no time to curl into a ball.

The bottle careened to the ground. Flung about, Jaz hoped she'd survive the fall. She slammed against the side and off again and then with an ear-splitting screech glass hit metal and her prison exploded.

As the glass flew, Jaz somersaulted away from the gleaming blade and landed on her side, cushioned by the soft tufts of the carpet. Winded but elated, she tried to catch her breath, and then heard a bell ringing and the rhythmic thudding of what sounded like giant footsteps.

As she tried to get to her feet, a massive furry paw knocked her down.

"Whisper!"

The bell around his neck chimed like a church bell. She stood again, but he swiped at her, flicking her from one paw to the other. She tried to crawl away but stopped short when his razor sharp claws slashed through the air and tore through her skirts, barely missing her thigh. He pinned her to the carpet.

"Whisper, it's me. Don't you recognise me."

He looked at her with his massive green eyes, but she saw no sign of recognition. His mouth opened wide, his white fangs flashing in the light. His head bent towards her. Jaz screamed and wriggled for all she was worth as he lifted her into his mouth.

Chapter Sixteen

Woken by a rumbling sound he couldn't place, Rick rubbed his eyes and looked around the strange room, at the shiny green walls and floor.

"Where on earth am I?" He stretched his spine, sat up and darted a glance over each shoulder, remembering being attacked by the scary creatures. They'd overcome him and now he appeared to be in some sort of prison. But where? It didn't look anything like Jaz's living room. And what had happened to Jaz? And what the hell were those damn things? He'd never heard of anything like them before, let alone encountered the like.

He could still hear the noise coming from outside the room. Head pounding, mouth dry, vision blurry he crawled to the edge of the room and tapped on the surface. "Glass? Really?"

He looked outside trying to locate the sound. He spotted the source. Surely he had to be dreaming. He rubbed his eyes again hardly able to believe what he was seeing. An enormous bottle was wobbling about right outside his room. A giant green wine bottle.

"Whoa! Weird."

He got to his feet, spun around, taking in his own predicament. "Shit! Shit! And double shit! I'm in a bloody bottle!"

Fuelled by panic, he banged his fists on the wall. "Let me out, you bastards. Let me out!"

Something glinting in the wobbling bottle caught his eye. He pressed his face closer against the glass, trying to make it out through the distortions of the coloured curved surface. The something raced across his line of vision, a dark creature, flashing spurts of light. It smashed into the side, the bottle picked up momentum and the creature ran back to the opposite side.

"My God! Sequins. Jaz! Jaz! It's me!" He hammered his fists and yelled with all his might as she launched herself at the side of the bottle.

His voice caught in his throat, his fists slamming to a halt as the bottle pitched over the side of the table, reminding him of a crazed vehicle plummeting over a cliff. His heart clenched. If the glass smashed she'd be cut to smithereens. The bottle exploded. Relief flooded his heart and he cheered as with the skill of an acrobat she managed to escape what he'd imagined to be certain death.

Rick spotted the gigantic furry beast before Jaz did.

"Jaz, watch out! Behind you! Fuck, she hasn't seen it. Jaz!"

Despite making as much noise as he could, it was obvious she couldn't hear him. Helpless, he watched her being scooped into its mouth and carried from the room.

"Bring her back. If you hurt one hair on her head, I'll kill you..."

He had to rescue her before she was eaten alive, and he'd need to arm himself. The cat terrified him; he'd no doubt that at his present size one slash of those mighty claws would shred him to ribbons. But first things first. He needed to find a way out.

Jaz had worked out how to upset her bottle, but he didn't rate his chances of being able to leap out of the way as successfully as she had. A spot of light was reflected in the centre of the glass floor. He looked up the neck of the bottle and realised it wasn't sealed. A way out if only he could get up there.

He searched his pockets, wishing he was in his work gear; then he'd have a Swiss army knife, some string and a pencil. Not that he knew what good they'd be, it wasn't like he could draw a door and walk out. Time was of the essence. He had no choice but to risk Jaz's strategy and hope for survival.

Following her example he ran at the wall and felt a thrill of satisfaction as the bottle began to move. Racing against time he repeated the effort until the bottle teetered, then toppled headlong into space. Rick forced his eyes open, preparing to look for a safe landing the second the glass smashed. His head slammed against the wall as the bottle landed intact and spun around. Ricocheted into the air he twisted and turned before landing on his back with a thud. He rubbed his head, wincing as an egg-shaped lump rose beneath his fingers, but he allowed himself a moment of triumph. The bottle lay on its side.

It rocked slightly as Rick walked over to the neck. He pushed his head and shoulders into the narrow tunnel and wriggled the rest of his body into the confined space. Progress was slow as he fought for purchase on the smooth sides but once his knees were inside he braced his back against the side and used his hands, elbows and knees to worm his way to the exit.

Panting, he poked his head out and gasped fresh air, and then he turned onto his stomach and surveyed the floor below. A couple of jagged slivers of glass from Jaz's bottle stuck out of the carpet waiting to pierce his flesh if he made a wrong move. He tried to create some momentum, gratified when the bottle pivoted enough to provide him with a soft landing. Bit by bit he lowered his upper body towards the floor until his hands sank into the soft wool carpet. A second later he dropped in a heap, jumped to his feet and looked around for a weapon with which to attack the cat and rescue Jaz.

Other than the broken glass the only thing he could see that might be of use was a drawing pin lying underneath the edge of the settee. He sprinted across to it. The pin was bent, but he could use it as a shield. He pulled off his shirt, stretched the fabric at the top of one sleeve over a piece of glass and dragging the fabric to and fro cut it off. He redressed in the one armed shirt and then wrapped the detached sleeve around one end of a shard of glass as long his forearm. Armed with his makeshift sword and shield Rick headed into battle.

Chapter Seventeen

Whisper trotted across the hall, his claws clicking a loud tattoo on the tiled floor. Jaz's surroundings blurred, and she fought a wave of nausea as he rounded the corner into the kitchen. His breath smelled of tuna fish and her stomach heaved.

"Whisper! Put me down!" He must know it was her, must recognise her scent, but he ignored her plea. She shuddered, visualising what he could do to mice. Now she'd be his next meal. Well, she hadn't gotten out of the bottle to be eaten by a cat—and not just any cat, her cat, her pet. The stray cat she had taken in and cared for, positively doted on. Never had a cat been more spoiled. The self same cat she had jumped into the wall to rescue. Did he remember that? He owed her one.

She had to be able to outwit him. Her head, arms and legs protruded from either side of his mouth. She reached up her hand, curled it round a whisker as thick as her finger and yanked on it, wriggling and kicking for all she was worth, hoping he'd open his mouth and drop her.

No such luck. Whisper made a sound deep in his throat and miaowed. His rough tongue grated against her bare midriff dragging on her skin and she let out a yelp of pain, but he didn't unclamp his jaw. As she squirmed from side to side his jaw tightened. She let her body go limp. The sharp edge of one of his teeth was pressing on her back, if it pierced her it would puncture a kidney, then she'd have no chance of escape.

He ducked his head and Jaz spotted the cat flap. Instinctively, she drew her knees upwards, covered her head with her arms and prepared for an impact that didn't eventuate. In one fluid motion Whisper tupped the flap open and bounded through the gap into fresh air. Behind them the flap rattled with the intensity of artillery fire before settling back into place.

If Jaz had been scared before, it was as nothing compared to the terror that gripped her now. The great outdoors. Being as tiny as Thumbalina in the house had been bad enough, but he could take her anywhere out here and she might not be able to find her way back, assuming she escaped. Even the garden with which she was familiar looked completely different from this vantage point.

Blades of grass pinged against her, stinging her flesh. A fly bigger than her head buzzed past and she buried her face in Whisper's fur. A breeze, like a gale, whipped her skirts into a frenzy flapping the layers of chiffon around Whisper's muzzle. He shook his head, paused, and then batted the fabric down with his paw. He glanced at a Red Admiral as it danced through the air towards the buddleia bush, then he picked up speed and Jaz jiggled in his grip, her arms and legs flailing in the air as the world rushed by.

She spotted the wheelbarrow and wondered where Ted was. She screamed his name on the off chance he might be around, might hear her, might see her. Whisper ducked under the wheelbarrow and her right foot dragged on the ground. Pain seared, she screwed up her eyes as red and black lights exploded behind her eyelids. She lifted her foot, and stuck her leg out in front, craning her neck in order to see the damage. A trickle of scarlet blood ran from her little toe where her nail had been torn off. A chunk of grey gravel had embedded itself in the edge of her foot. She rubbed at it with her other foot and managed to dislodge the stone.

Whisper slowed his pace as they approached the painting studio. The door stood open, and Jaz wondered who had unlocked it, she thought she remembered locking it. Maybe not. No matter, she'd more important things to worry about.

Whisper crouched on the ground, he opened his mouth, pushed his tongue against Jaz and she slid out. Before she could stand he pinned her down with a heavy paw. His tongue flicked around his mouth, then his head sank over her legs, fangs gleaming. Jaz thrashed, beat her tiny fists on his massive paw to no avail.

Whisper licked the blood off her toe and purred.

This was it.

The end.

She was going to be eaten alive. Tears of fear flooded from Jaz's eyes, snot poured from her nose and she whimpered.

And then he stopped licking her foot.

He rolled her onto her back and brought his face towards hers. She froze, her body rigid as her brain raced, finding nothing to cling to, nothing to offer hope or comfort. His mouth opened wide and she stared into the dark cavern of his throat. God, make it quick, make it painless. As his mouth sank towards her, Jaz closed her eyes, her body trembled as wave after wave of dread swelled through her.

Tears mingled with snot acted as a lubricant, as like an old bath towel, rough from years of use, his coarse tongue licked her cheek. He purred as he washed her clean, and with a blinding flash she realised she wasn't being treated as prey. She was being treated as a kitten, carried away from danger, washed and cared for. But wasn't that what she cats did, not tom's? Who cared as long as he didn't eat her?

Even though the licking sensation wasn't particularly pleasant, Jaz relaxed as the tension drained away and her heartbeat and breathing returned to normal.

When he had finished his ministrations, Whisper released her. She sat up, examined her foot, cringed at the sight of her mangled toe, but at least it had stopped bleeding and Whisper had done a good job of cleaning the wound.

She stood up. He bent his head and purred. She stroked his nose. "Thank you. You did good."

She looked around the studio, and remembered the spider webs. Her nerves were so jangled she'd probably die of fright if she saw a giant spider.

"What now?" she asked. She looked at Whisper. "We need to rescue Rick. He's trapped in a bottle too. We can't leave him there. We have to go back."

Jaz took a step towards the door. Whisper batted her down and she banged her elbow.

"Oh, come on! Enough of that." She stood up and rubbed her arm. "Have you got a better idea?"

"Miaow, miaow."

"Well, I wish I spoke more cat." She walked towards the chair and leant against its leg. It felt as sturdy as a tree trunk. Suddenly weary, she slid down to the floor and sat with her back against the chair leg. She ran a hand through her hair, her fingers caught in a tangle of knots.

Whisper sat in front of her, his head cocked to one side.

"Do you have any idea what's going on around here? First there's dissolving walls, and a secret room. Then slap bang in the middle of the house I've a stinky green well that makes noises. I've been attacked by scary monsters, and finally I've been shrunk. What the hell is going to happen next?"

In a blur of fur, Whisper once more scooped her into his mouth.

"Oh, not again. Now what?" Resigned to him being in charge she let her body go limp.

He walked around in a circle miaowing. She'd no idea what he was trying to tell her. Crouching low, he tilted his head and looked upwards. She could feel the tension in his body, his body taut as a bowstring, then a tremble, almost a bounce. He sprung into the air. Jaz's stomach plummeted, and a scream froze in her throat. They were airborne.

He landed softly on the chair, and plopped her onto the cushion, then he jumped back down to the floor.

She crawled to the edge of the seat and looked over the edge.

"Whisper! Where are you going? Come back. Don't leave me here. I can't get down."

He turned in the doorway, gave a final miaow, then tail aloft he strutted out.

Chapter Eighteen

With lungs threatening to explode and his heart beating wildly, Rick reached the cat flap. His legs shook beneath him and he slumped against the threshold gasping for breath, rubbing at the stitch in his side. He couldn't remember when he'd last run anywhere. He'd heard the cat flap rattle and figured the cat had taken Jaz outdoors. The feline could move much faster than he, and some cats roamed quite a distance in a day. They could be anywhere by now. He was on a hopeless quest, but if he didn't try to save her he'd be unable to live with himself. He put down his sword and shield.

On tiptoes, he stretched upwards and pushed the swing door of the cat flap. It hardly moved. He needed more leverage, to be higher. He looked around, spotted the bowl of water for the cat and thought he'd be able to balance on its thick rim. He wedged himself between the cupboard and bowl, put his shoulder to the rim and using the cupboard for purchase, pushed, almost falling as the bowl shot across the tiled floor. Water sloshed over the side wetting him. He flicked the water off his hair and face and then with much grunting manoeuvred the bowl into position. Setting the sword and shield on the broad rim he hoisted himself up. This time when he pressed, the door opened more, he held it ajar and looked outside. He couldn't see the cat.

Rick dropped the shield outside, it spun around before being brought up short beside the smiling faces of a clump of violas poking from a crack in the paving. He considered his sword. The glass would smash if he dropped it, he'd have to climb down with it in his hand. Careful not to slice himself with its sharp side he lay on the edge of the opening, legs dangling outside. The cat flap pressed heavily on his back, and he tried to alleviate the pain by inching through the gap. As soon as his head cleared the flap he dropped to the ground, managing to land squarely on his feet, the undamaged sword held at arm's length.

He snatched up the shield and began to jog down the path, leaping over the nicks, all the while searching for signs of Jaz. He dodged around a platoon of ants, and then slid through a snail trail, fought for balance and somehow avoided landing in the silvery slime.

He paused and with his hands cupped around his mouth called, "Jaz. Where are you? Can you hear me?"

Only birdsong and buzzing replied. He'd no idea where to go; the vastness of the garden and the towering vegetation overwhelmed him. She could be anywhere.

As he contemplated where to look next, a wasp jetted by, twisted in the air and returned for a better look. Terrified, Rick ducked, held the shield over his head and stabbed the sword towards his attacker. Buzzing angrily, the wasp darted back and forth. In his tiny state, Rick knew that a wasp sting would be fatal. He shrank behind the shield, his bicep trembling as he thrust it forward, up and down, parrying the blows as the wasp batted against it time and time again. Under the onslaught, he staggered backwards coming up hard against a rock—or maybe a pebble—it didn't matter which. Outwitted by an insect. Trapped. As the wasp made another furious foray towards the shield he mustered his courage, sidestepped, and using as much force as he could, plunged his blade deep into the stripy belly.

"Take that, you evil sod!"

He twisted the sword. The wasp jerked away, the embedded sword wrenched from Rick's hand and he stumbled to the ground. Wings glinting in the sunlight, the wasp spiralled down. Rick scuttled backwards on his bottom, avoiding the stinger as the angry insect crashed to earth and landed on the sword. The shriek of shattering glass mingled with the death throes of his adversary's final buzz.

Rick wiped the sweat from his forehead with the back of his wrist, and wondered what else he'd have to contend with. On jelly legs he searched the immediate vicinity for a new weapon. Finding nothing suitable he hefted a couple of pieces of gravel up and put one in each of his pockets, and then shield in hand, resumed his mission.

Chapter Nineteen

Jaz tried to stand but sank up to her knees as the soft cushion gave beneath her feet. She crawled to the edge of the seat and looked at the ground. Far too far to jump.

"How the hell am I going to get down?"

If she could slide down a chair leg she might be able to get back to the house and Rick. She squashed down her rising anxiety as she thought about the evil creatures that had overpowered them. What were they, and what did they want? She wished she'd never found the secret room and knocked the wall down. Whoever had bricked it up must have encountered the scary creatures. She wondered whether they'd returned to search for someone else and she'd gotten in the way.

Holding onto the cushion she peered over the edge of the chair and realised the legs were set in from the edge of the seat. Damn! The smooth overhang looked impossible to safely traverse. She sat up and plucked at the cushion fabric contemplating her dilemma. Damn Whisper for putting her up here. If she wanted to be a prisoner she'd have stayed in the bottle. Well, she'd managed to find a way out of that, and she'd find one down to terra firma. Whisper had underestimated her if he thought she'd stay put.

Jaz fingered the piping cord trim on the cushion. The faded twisted silk threads made a rope as thick as her wrist. A rope! She scooted around the edge of the cushion until she found the cord's starting point. Held in place by a tidy slipstitch, the thread attaching cord to cushion unpicked easily. Whenever the thread became too long to handle easily she gnawed at it with her teeth and snapped it off, dragging the rope away from the edge.

Finally, with the rope free, she held an end and began coiling it from hand to elbow and back again. By the time she was halfway through, her shoulder and arm ached from the weight and she dragged the remainder behind her as she staggered over the soft slopes of the cushion. She reached the rear of the seat, and sank to her knees, dropping the heavy coil, and then she tied one end around one of the upright back slats. She grabbed the rope between both hands, dug her heels into the cushion and leant back, tugging hard to check the security of the knot. Satisfied with her effort, she tossed the free end of the rope over the edge of the chair, smiling as she watched it unfurl.

A small cloud of dust rose as the free end of rope plopped on the floor, and pooled around. Heart in her mouth, Jaz put her feet on either side of the rope, gripped it tightly and inched backwards to the edge of the seat. She looked down and her resolve wavered. Her guts clenched. The paint, spattered stone floor, such a long, long way down, offered a rock-hard landing. If she fell, her leg or her neck might break. She squashed down her fear, took a deep breath and stepped into space.

The rope swung. Eyes closed, she clung tight. Her chiffon skirts slid against the silky rope providing little friction, and she began to slide. She clenched her thighs tighter, and used her bare hands and feet to slow her descent, dreading the rope burn if she lost control and slid too fast. Her shoulders and biceps burned with the effort.

Relief swept through Jaz when her feet hit the ground. She released her grip on the rope and straightened her clothes, noticing that one of her delicate chiffon skirts had been torn and begun to fray. A tinkling bell sounded. She darted behind the chair leg and turned her attention to the doorway.

Whisper trotted into the room. She stepped from her hiding place and he stopped dead. A small growl rumbled deep in his throat as he glanced up at the seat then back at her. Jaz pulled herself up to her full height, only a few centimetres she realised, and placed her hands on her hips.

"Well, what did you expect?" she asked. "I didn't know if you were coming back. I can't sit around here all day. I need to get back to the house and rescue Rick."

Whisper swished his tail and miaowed loudly. Jaz began walking towards the door, but stopped in her tracks. The doorway filled with light announcing Balmanza's arrival. A glowing ball of orange light tinged with aquamarine, he entered the room and shot around the periphery.

She rolled her eyes and shook her head. "Great, that's all I need. A hyperactive genie whizzing around the place."

The ball of light circled her before coming to a halt beside Whisper. "Got yourself into a bit of a mess, I see," said Balmanza.

Jaz crossed her arms. "It was those monsters from the well. They attacked me and Rick and shrunk us. What the hell are they? I assume *you* know."

"Of course I know. They come from the beginning of time. They want the key."

"What key?"

"*THE* key." A rainbow of colour flashed around Balmanza's middle. He was obviously pleased with himself.

"Stop showing off," she scolded. "You've lost me. I've no idea what you're talking about."

"It's the key to the box."

"What box?" She tapped the side of her head "Once again. I'm lost. Any chance you could tell me the whole story rather than turning this into a game of twenty questions? Assume I know nothing."

"Not a difficult assumption to make, Lightning."

Ooh! What she wouldn't like to do to that arrogant, good- for-nothing streak of fire. She bit her tongue. She was in enough trouble without pissing off a genie.

"Are you sure you want the whole story?" he asked.

"Yes."

"You might want to sit down. It'll take two hours."

Whisper lay down and rested his head on his paws, his eyes fixed on the genie.

Jaz stamped her foot; she'd no intention of sitting down. "Two hours! I haven't got two hours to waste. I need to find Rick, and then get rid of the monsters. Give me the highlights, quick as you can."

"If you insist."

"I do, I do. For heaven's sake, get on with it."

"Very well. Back at the beginning of time there were two boxes. One held all the bad, evil things in the world and the other held all the good things. One day a young woman found the box of good things. She couldn't open the locked box, but she burned to know what was inside. She tried to break it open, without success. The box had a lock, and for many years she searched and searched for a key that would reveal the box's secret. When she was a wizened old woman she found the key. The minute the tumblers released, the lid sprung open and the box released its bounty. Out flew: love, kindness, peace, joy, tenderness, caring. You name it, all the goodness flew into the world."

"Like Pandora's box — only her box had evil stuff."

"Exactly. You're not as dumb as you look, Lightning."

Jaz bristled. The cheek of him! Before she had chance to tear him off a strip or two Whisper stood and flicked her with his tail before standing beside her.

"Pandora had one box, and Aisha had the other," continued Balmanza.

Jaz gasped. "*Aisha*?"

"Yes, Aisha."

The little hairs on the back of Jaz's neck rose and goosebumps raced along her arms. "And what has this got to do with me?" she whispered.

"The crails want the key back." Balmanza turned a dark shade of purple, almost black. "They want to put all the good things back in the box."

"Who are the crails?"

"The ones you call monsters. You have the key. They want it. Their only purpose is to find the key. They'll destroy whatever they have to in order to secure its return."

"I don't have the damn key. Why do they assume I have? Why pick on me? Why are they in my house?"

Whisper nuzzled Jaz, almost knocking her over. He licked the scar tissue on her shoulder with his rough tongue. She appreciated his attempt to comfort her, but tried to discourage him, as she listened to Balmanza's explanation.

"Your house is built on the intersection of important lay lines, the perfect place for a portal. After countless millennia of searching the crails have found you. You're the descendent of Aisha, you even carry her name."

Jaz shook her head. "Not really. I picked the name off a list because it sounded pretty. Lots of people are called Aisha."

"But you are her descendent."

"You're joking, right?"

"Wrong. Your name means life. The things in the box make life worth living."

"There's got to be a mistake. Tell them. It's not me they're looking for."

"It is. It was predicted."

Jaz rubbed her forehead. "What else is in the prediction?"

"You don't want to know."

She sighed. "You're right, I probably don't, but tell me anyway."

Balmanza flashed his colours at Whisper. The cat miaowed, stretched and flexed his claws.

"There will be a battle to the death."

"Oh, shit! You mean I'm going to die? Couldn't you have dressed it up a bit? I'm no match for those bloody things. What if I run away?"

"They'll find you. You released them and now they have your scent. They'll not stop chasing you until you hand over the key."

How the hell had she landed in such a mess? She chewed on her nail, looking from the genie to Whisper and back again. "There's got to be a way to make them go away?"

"There is. I told you. Give them the key."

"But I haven't got it," she shouted, and stamped her foot. "I haven't damn well got it. Anyway, even if I had I wouldn't want to give it to them, not if they'd take all the good things away."

"Then you'd better prepare for a fight."

With his nose, Whisper pushed Jaz nearer to Balmanza. She tried to resist and move away, but Whisper slapped a paw on the hem of her skirt. She tugged at the fabric, but Whisper held tight.

"Let me go!"

Whisper bared his teeth, and she shrank back, releasing the tension in the chiffon. He cocked his head at Balmanza and miaowed several times. She wished she knew what he was saying. He moved away from Jaz, but before she could dash away, Balmanza shifted shape. Stretching into a long oval of blue, red and orange flames he spiralled around her until she was fully encased in a flickering wall of colour. She clutched at her throat, turning in a circle looking for a way out, but Balmanza swirled quicker and quicker until the colours merged into an iridescent blur. Her hair rose in the draft he created and then, unbidden, her arms lifted above her head. Layer after layer of chiffon flapped around her as her feet left the ground and she levitated in mid-air. Jaz tried to scream, but no noise came from her throat. Nausea swept through her as she floated higher and higher, defying gravity, her body corkscrewing around and around. She glanced at the ground only a metre or so below, but in her diminutive state it looked like a gaping chasm. If Balmanza released her she'd plummet to earth and be dashed to death on the stone floor.

Her motion slowed, Balmanza came closer and enveloped her in his bands of pulsating energy. At last, Jaz found her vocal chords and let loose an ear-piercing scream. Searing pain shot through her muscles. Balamanza eased away and lowered her to the ground. The instant her soles slapped on the cool stone floor the pain evaporated and the scream died on her lips. Balmanza gathered himself back into a ball. Jaz rubbed her eyes, looked at Whisper, at the room, and at herself.

"Oh my God! I'm normal size again. Thank you, thank you. I thought you were going to kill me. You're the best genie in the world."

"I know." Balmanza flashed his rainbow effect again. "But you should be thanking my master. He commanded it."

Jaz picked up Whisper and stroked his head. She looked into his big green eyes and smiled. "You're the best cat ever. I'll open a tin of red salmon for you for your tea."

Whisper purred, and rubbed his cheek against her arm.

"Okay, first priority: we get Rick out of his bottle. Then we work out what to do with the crails."

Whisper hopped to the ground and together they ran into the garden. Jaz spotted Millie running through the rose garden.

"Jasmy, Jasmy we been looking for you. Ooh, you look like a fairy princess."

"Hi, Millie." Jaz looked over her shoulder, Balmanza had disappeared.

"Gwanddad, I founded her," called Millie. She tried to pick Whisper up, but he'd experienced Millie's hugs before and shot under a thorny rose bush where she couldn't reach.

"Ah, there you are, Jasmine." Hoe in hand, Ted caught up with Millie. "There's a woman from the art gallery here to see you. I hope you don't mind, I put her in the living room."

"Err, yeah, that's fine." Except it wasn't fine, Rick was in there, in a bottle. She'd no idea how to explain to Ted what had been happening, and she didn't want to scare Millie with tales of monsters who could shrink a person to the size of Thumbelina. It was easier to say nothing.

Ted looked her up and down, and frowned. "Are you doing a show today? If so you might want to look in a mirror."

She glanced down at herself and saw streaks of dirt and a couple of bloody scratches. "No. No show." She set off at a run, hoping Annabel wouldn't spot Rick. "I'll go and see what Annabel wants."

She opened the back door and kicked Whisper's water bowl across the room. "What the hell...?"

She picked up the bowl and put it in the sink ready for washing and refilling, then went to the living room to see Annabel. Annabel wasn't there. Relieved at not having to explain about Rick being shrunk to fit into a bottle, Jaz dashed into the room and squatted by the coffee table. No bottles. Her heart squeezed. She scanned the floor, seeing her sword, broken glass and an intact bottle. She snatched up the bottle, held it to the light and gasped. No Rick. Where had he gone? Had the crails returned for him or had he managed to escape? She hoped for the latter. She put the bottle on the table, and careful to avoid the broken glass, lay on her belly and searched under the sofa and chairs, calling, "Rick, are you there? It's me, Jaz."

Stretching as far as she could reach, she slid her hand under each piece of furniture, slowly brushing the carpet with her fingers. No Rick.

Her stomach churned with fear. The crails could be torturing him right now, trying to discover the whereabouts of the key. He wouldn't have a clue what they wanted, and be helpless against them. Sour bile rose and burnt her throat. She swallowed it down and stood up, wondering what to do next. If he had managed to escape where would he be and how far could he travel on his own two tiny feet? She glanced round the room, checking she hadn't missed anywhere he might be hiding, and then through the window she spotted a shiny black BMW on the drive. Annabel's. Still here, then.

Keeping her eyes on the ground and scanning from side to side looking for Rick, Jaz stepped into the hallway, and noticed the library door was ajar. Since the crails had made their presence known, she had developed a fear of the room.

Terrified that Annabel had become their next victim, she paused outside the door, her hand hovering above the handle. She had to go in and check. The putrid essence from the well, so thick she could almost taste it, oozed from the room, assaulting her nostrils. She wrinkled her nose, trying not to breathe any more than she had to.

"Stop wasting time," she chided herself. "In. Now."

Screwing up her courage, she willed herself forward, and with her heart threatening to burst from her chest, pushed the door open.

Impeccably clad in a black trouser suit, Annabel crouched on the floor rifling through the piles of books and artefacts.

Jaz let out a sigh of relief. "There you are." Thank God, nothing had happened to her.

Annabel flashed her toothpaste advert smile, gleaming white teeth framed by cherry red lips. "Sorry for dropping in without an appointment. I was in the area."

"Great. Sorry about the mess." Jaz edged around a pile of leather bound manuscripts and bent down, pretending to unplug a standard lamp, her gaze scouring the room, looking for Rick. Satisfied he wasn't there, she stood up. "I'm renovating."

"No problem. I've been looking through these treasures. A fascinating collection. I adore old books and ancient artefacts." She looked Jaz up and down and frowned. "Have you been partying? Nice costume. Fancy dress?"

"No. I'm a belly dancer. Give me a minute while I change. You might be more comfortable in the kitchen. It's a lot cleaner and a damn sight less smelly."

Annabel turned her attention to the next pile. "It smells fine to me."

Jaz blinked in disbelief. Her stomach griped at the stench, even stronger in the room than in the hallway. She looked at the gaping hole in the wall, the green glow from the well a much deeper and more intense hue than she remembered. Fingers of phosphorescence reached along the ground and up the walls of the hidden room. Silken walls of newly woven spider webs stretched from the well to the piles of rubble. From the depths noise rumbled, and a voice whispered, "Aisha," freezing the blood in Jaz's veins.

Fixated by the library's treasures, Annabel seemed oblivious to it all. Jaz shifted her weight from foot to foot, unsure what to do. The well must be the portal Balmanza had mentioned. She wondered if the crails had returned to wherever they'd come from, and whether all manner of scary creatures were lined up waiting to hurtle through time and space into her library. She didn't want Annabel to end up a crail victim.

"I'd rather you waited in the kitchen," she said.

Annabel's eyes narrowed as she looked at Jaz, then she rose and dusted off her trouser suit. "If you insist."

She picked her way through the cascades of books and reached the door. Jaz closed it tight and showed Annabel to the kitchen.

She could barely concentrate on Annabel's conversation about the forthcoming art extravaganza. Where the hell was Rick? She went to the sink, rinsed Whisper's water bowl and refilled it, and remembered it had been by the back door. She hefted it. Could he have moved it? Why? She put the bowl on the ground, but other than a few splashes of water on the tiles nothing was out of kilter. She returned to the sink, picked up the kettle, removed the lid and made sure he wasn't inside before filling it with water and switching it on. She pointed to the cups. "Help yourself to some tea or coffee. I won't be long."

Chapter Twenty

Riding on the adrenalin surge from killing the mighty wasp, Rick jogged through the garden swinging his shield, his gaze flicking one way and then the other looking for signs of Jaz. Agile as a goat, he leapt from rock to rock, ducked under low leaves and dodged flower stems. The sun beat down and sweat dripped down his back. Beneath the wheelbarrow he paused and wiped his brow, thankful for a moment's shade. The shield clattered when he discarded it. Hands on thighs, he bent over and drew in a couple of deep breaths.

"Shit!"

He dropped to his knees and touched the wet centre of a dark patch on the gravel. His fingers came away red, he sniffed them. Blood. He knew it had to be Jaz's.

His heart plummeted and he slumped against one of the wheelbarrow's legs and wiped the blood on his trousers. "Oh, God! Don't let that cat have eaten her, please don't let him have eaten her."

Rick snatched up the shield, stepped out of the shade and clambered up a rise. He yelled at the top of his voice. "Jaz! Jaz!"

He listened for a response, but all he could hear were birds singing and insects buzzing. In the distance he spotted

Whisper trotting across the garden. No Jaz. He ran towards the cat, but couldn't catch him.

"If you've hurt her, I'll kill you." He shook his fist at Whisper's back. The cat showed no sign of having seen or heard him and carried on his journey. "What have you done with her?"

It was too horrible to contemplate her having been eaten by her own cat. He refused to believe it and pushed the thought from his mind. Half crazed with worry and with no clear plan Rick set off running again. He looked behind planters and under fallen leaves, all the time calling her name.

His pace slowed as he stepped onto straw, piled in small hillocks. He sniffed the air, and salivated. Strawberries. He could smell the warm, sweetness of them. Suddenly, he was starving. He looked up. On the ridge of the hillocks he could see them, giant red balls nestled beneath dark green leaves. He hauled himself through the loose straw and into the strawberry patch. The plump, ripe fruit stretched in all directions, the berries dwarfing him. He wandered around a plant until he found a small berry, his arms could barely reach around it and he feared if he yanked it off the plant its momentum might cause them both to roll back down the hillock. Crushed to death by a strawberry. The absurdity of it struck him as funny and he chuckled to himself.

He sat on one leaf under the shade of another and sank his teeth into his chosen berry. Sticky juice ran down his chin and dripped onto his chest as the sweet flesh satiated his hunger. His leg muscles began to ache. He felt like he'd run for miles and exhaustion set in. He couldn't carry on running blindly round the garden hoping to find Jaz. He needed to be more organised, more systematic. He leant against a stem and closed his eyes, for a second, whilst he decided what to do next.

* * *

Rick awoke with a start. He'd no idea how long he'd been asleep, but judging by the position of the sun he figured it couldn't have been long. He wondered what had awoken him and looked around.

He heard a high voice singing, something about ducks swimming. He looked in the direction of the sound and saw a lime green bucket swinging from one hand of a giant skipping towards the strawberry patch. He'd seen her once or twice before but only at a distance. Ted's granddaughter...what was her name...Molly...no, Millie. Rick held his breath as the massive feet encased in sparkly pink sandals came closer. He thought about making a dash for it, but what if she changed direction and he ended up squashed like chewing gum to the sole of her shoe? No, he'd stay put and wait until she'd gone past before he moved on.

But Millie didn't move on. She stopped. Still singing about the ducks, she put her bucket on the ground between Rick's strawberry plant and the next and began picking berries. She dropped one in the bucket and one into her mouth.

"Yummy for my tummy," she giggled and rubbed her belly with one hand and bit into another strawberry.

She stripped the first plant of its offerings, each one thudding into the bucket or disappearing into Millie's mouth. She moved onto Rick's plant, the leaves shook as she tugged at the first berry. Rick crawled deeper into the plant and came face to face with a snail. It flicked its antenna and opened its jaw. Before he could stop himself, Rick screamed, backing away as fast as he could.

He scrambled to his feet and began to run down the side of the hillock. His feet slid beneath him and he tumbled over, rolling head over heels. He heard the stomp of giant feet, a shadow blocked the sun and then a pair of enormous hands came down and encased him. The world spun and his stomach lurched as he moved faster than an elevator from the ground to Millie's chest level. Millie opened her hands and peered in at her find.

"Hello," she said. "I'm Millie. Are you a faiwy?"

"No, I'm Rick."

A finger and thumb around his waist she picked him up and turned him from side to side. "You haven't got wings."

"I'm not a fairy."

Millie scratched her head. "You must be a pixie then. Why haven't you got pointy ears?"

"I just haven't."

"You're all pink."

Rick looked at his shirt and pants. "It's strawberry juice."

"I like stwawbewies. They're yummy for my tummy." She jumped up and down.

Each vertebra in Rick's spine crunched and his teeth rattled. "Less jumping, please."

"Don't you like to jump? I do. I'm good at it. I can jump as high as a house. Watch me."

"Put me down so I can watch."

"Okay." She sat him on the rim of the bucket.

Half expecting her to have super powers, he clung to the edge and watched as Millie leapt into the air. She managed to clear a strawberry plant. He clapped. "Fantastic. You're an excellent jumper."

"Where do you live?" she asked, sitting cross-legged on the ground.

"Not here. I'm a little lost."

"You can stay in the faiwy house."

"Where's that?"

"I'll take you," she said, plonking him on top of the strawberries.

"Don't swing the bucket," he said, clutching his stomach as she swung it forward. "If you do I'll be sick on your strawberries."

"Yucky."

Millie walked a few steps and stopped, lowering the bucket to the ground. Rick balanced on a massive strawberry and looked over the rim. In front of him was a house made of golden sandstone, complete with windows, a dark green door and a chimney pot.

"It's the faiwy house," said Millie. "The tooth faiwy lives here. You can stay with her."

Millie bent over and tapped on the door. Rick wouldn't have been surprised if the tooth fairy had answered it. Millie leant on her side and looked through a window.

"She's not home, but you can stay." She pushed open the door and put Rick on the path. "You can have the wittle bedwoom. Go on in."

She prodded his back and having no option he entered the house. It could have been made for him. A table and chairs his size, a sofa and a rocking chair, and a piano. He looked into the other rooms: a bathroom and two bedrooms with four-poster beds. If worst came to worst, he could live quite happily here, he thought.

All of a sudden, a loud rumbling noise thundered and he ran towards the front door. The room flooded with light from above. He looked up; the roof had gone. Millie looked in.

"There you are," she laughed, and scooped him into her hand. "Do you like it?"

"It's wonderful."

"Nanalu made it for Jasmy's gwandma. Do you know Jasmy?"

"Yes. I'm trying to find her."

"I know where she is."

"Thank God!" Rick held out his palms. "Is she all right? When did you see her?"

"Befowe."

"When before?"

"Befowe now. Can you do magic?"

"Only a couple of card tricks."

"I like magic. If you had some fairy dust you could make me fly." She curled her fingers around Rick, letting his head poke out of her fist, then sticking her arms out at shoulder level she flapped her arms and spun around pretending to be a bird.

Rick screamed, swearing he'd never again go on a white-knuckle ride. His stomach performed somersaults, and his vision blurred. The more he screamed, the faster she flapped her arms. "Stop for Christ's sake. Bloody hell, you're killing me."

Millie stopped. Held him close to her face and frowned, her face coming in and out of focus as he tried to stop the world spinning.

"You said naughty words. You a bad pixie."

"Sorry. You scared me."

"Your face is a funny colour."

"I'm not surprised." Rick rubbed his eyes. "Will you take me to Jaz...Jasmy?"

"No. You mine."

"Jasmy will be worried about me."

Millie's eyes widened. "Will she?"

"Yes." He had to find the words to persuade her to fetch Jaz. Together they could work out the best way to proceed. Rick stood in the centre of Millie's palm, and gave her his most serious look. "Millie, this is most important. I need you to do something very grown-up. Can you do that?"

Wide-eyed, she nodded hard enough to make her curls bounce.

"If you won't take me to Jasmy, you must find her and bring her here. Tell her Rick sent you. Can you do that?"

"Yes."

"Good girl."

"Millie, where are you?" Ted's voice carried across the garden. "It's time to go."

"Hush." Millie put a finger to her lips, and then she put Rick inside the house.

"Get Jasmy," Rick implored.

Millie put the roof on and closed the front door.

"I'm here, Gwanddad," she called.

"Get Jasmy!"

Chapter Twenty-One

Jaz raced upstairs and changed into a pair of shorts and a T-shirt. A headache throbbed behind her forehead. She pressed on her temples, knowing it would do no good. The day had become stifling, hot and humid, making her skin sticky. She glanced at her grubby face in the bathroom mirror, scrubbed away the dirt, washed her hands and dragged a brush through her hair deciding that was as good as it was going to get. Annabel couldn't have picked a more inopportune moment to call, the sooner she left the better, then Jaz could continue her search for Rick. She hoped he had found a safe hiding place, hoped the crails hadn't come back and found him, and wrought more havoc on him.

In the kitchen, Annabel had made a pot of tea. *No sign of her leaving soon, then.* Jaz's stomach rumbled. She opened a packet of custard creams and ate three one after the other. "So what can I do for you?" she asked, offering the opened packet to her guest.

Annabel waved the biscuits aside and put down her cup. "I was hoping I could take the glass bottle today, and maybe some of the other artefacts your mother used as motifs in her paintings."

"I'm sorry, I had an accident with the bottle. It shattered into a thousand pieces."

Annabel's head jerked up, her eyes widened. She snarled. "You broke the bottle!"

Taken aback by Annabel's anger, Jaz blanched. "I know you wanted it for the exhibition, but there are other bottles you could pick from. There are some lovely alternatives on Nanalu's shelves. You can take whichever you like. Mum painted lots of them."

Her beautiful face becoming hard, Annabel glared. "But that one was special."

A shard of ice inched down Jaz's spine. She wondered if Annabel knew about Balmanza, but how could she? Nobody knew until Whisper tripped her and she released the genie. Maybe Whisper had known, but only because he was a cat with a destiny. Even now only she and Whisper knew the secret of the bottle.

"Well, it's gone now. Nothing to be done about it. Anyway, I don't know why you're so bothered. It was my bottle. I'm the one who should be upset or angry about it, not you." Her headache ratcheted up a notch and she screwed her eyes against a blinding stab of pain. Her suffering intense, she looked in the pantry, scrabbled through an ice-cream tub filled with throat lozenges, cough medicine and left over prescriptions, but no painkillers. None. She closed the pantry door, leant back on it and rubbed her forehead. Where the hell were they? She scanned the room. Handbag! The bag dangled from the back of a kitchen chair. Desperate for something to alleviate her suffering, she tipped the contents onto the table sifted through until her fingers settled on the strip of painkillers. She popped a couple from the blister pack, swilling them down with the dregs of her tea.

"Jasmy, Jasmy. Where are you?" Millie's voice came from the garden.

Jaz opened the door. "I'm here. What's wrong?"

Millie burst into the room, grabbed Jaz's hand and tugged on it. "You have to come now."

"In a minute. I've got a friend here."

Millie hid behind Jaz's leg, still pulling her hand. "You've got to come now. Not in a minute."

"Millie, be patient."

"No, now!"

What's wrong with her? Normally so well behaved. Jaz crouched to Millie's level. "You're being terribly rude."

"Sowwy." Millie pouted, then edged towards the table, her eyes lighting up when they saw the contents of Jaz's bag. She reached into the pile of offerings and picked up the rubber-encased phone. " Ooh, can I call my pixie?"

"No!" Jaz removed the phone from Millie's fingers and dropped it into her handbag.

Millie pouted, but then her eyes spotted a new treasure. "Spawkly."

Scared that Millie might hurt herself on the letter opener, Jaz took it from her. "No, you can't play with that. You might cut yourself."

Annabel put down her cup. "What's that?"

"My letter opener." She held it aloft.

A smile curled at the corner of Annabel's mouth and her eyes gleamed. She reached out, but before she could take it, Millie grabbed Jaz's wrist and jumped up and down. Jaz switched the opener to her other hand and slipped it into her pocket.

"Millie, calm down."

"You have to come. I fowgot. It's 'powtant." Using both hands she yanked on Jaz's arm.

"Later."

"Now, Jasmy, now." She stamped her foot, her cheeks flushed. "I've found a pixie. He's called Wic."

Jaz gasped. Tried to make light of the situation. She rolled her eyes at Annabel and smiled. "I'm sorry. I'll not get any peace until I go with her. We'll do this another time. Perhaps you could see yourself out."

Chapter Twenty-Two

Rick pressed his face against the window of the fairy house and watched Millie disappear from sight. His fate lay in the hands of a young child. How old was she? Three? Four at most. He rubbed his hand across his stubble and paced from room to room.

The thick sandstone walls repelled the heat of the day, but the humidity crept in, coating his skin in a clammy film. He noticed the patch of blood he'd wiped on his jeans and shuddered. Despite having seen Whisper carry Jaz away, he balked at the idea of her being dead. The chance she'd survived an attack by the cat might be slim, but until he saw evidence to the contrary he had to believe she was alive. He didn't want to deal with the alternative. Clever and resourceful, she'd somehow have gotten away. Surely?

Now she'd have to survive all the perils of the garden, not just the cat. Ted did a great job of keeping it in order, but for Rick the fearful jungle held new terrors lurking at every turn. Being on home turf, didn't guarantee Jaz's safety. He hoped she'd found a safe place to hide, and equally hoped she hadn't moved since Millie had last seen her. If she'd gone walkabout, the child might not find her.

Thirst struck. Parched, Rick went to the kitchen sink for a drink, but the taps, carved from wood and painted silver, yielded nothing. He banged his hand on the counter. "Damn and blast!"

Through the kitchen window, not too far away, he spotted a garden hose snaking along the ground. Ted must have been watering the plants. As he watched, a drop of water bulged from the end of the hose, trembled for a second, then breaking free exploded on the ground and seeped into the soil. He ran his tongue over his dry lips. Cool, clear water. Waiting for him.

He'd promised Millie he'd stay in the house, but his thirst raged, his throat yearning for a drink. Now he'd seen the water he had to have it. Besides, he could be back here before she returned. She could be ages, assuming she even remembered her mission. With his minimal knowledge of small children he'd no idea whether she'd carry out the task or become side tracked and forget all about him. How long should he give her before he took matters into his own hands? He watched another droplet ease its way from the hose, and decided to go. He couldn't let dehydration set in, or his decision-making ability would be shot to hell.

The fairy house front door, which Millie had released with ease, took all his strength to open. Outside warm air enveloped and oppressed him, and the water's lure became stronger. He left the door wide open and jogged to the hose. The oasis. A breeze moved over the damp earth and acted like air conditioning cooling his hot skin. He pushed his eager lips against the rim of the hose as a fat droplet squeezed its way out. He sucked on it and waited for the next one to form. When he'd drunk his fill, he bent over and let the water splash his head and neck, moving so it could trickle down his back and chest.

In the distance he heard the faint rumble of thunder and looked up at the sky, spotting a bank of black clouds building on the horizon. Not wanting to be outside in a storm, where a heavy deluge might carry him away, he took a last gulp of water and headed back to the safety of the fairy house.

Chapter Twenty-Three

"Where do you think you're going, young lady?" Ted brought the wheelbarrow full of tools to a stop, blocking Jaz and Millie's path. He handed Jaz a lettuce and a tub of blackcurrants. "That's the last of the blackcurrants."

"Gwandad, I have to show Jasmy something 'powtant."

"Not now you don't."

"But..."

"No buts. It's almost time to go."

Millie looked from Ted to Jaz and back again. "I have to show Jasmy the pixie."

"Another time."

"No." She put her hands on her hips and stamped her foot. "Now. I have to do it now."

Jaz intervened. Millie having a full-blown tantrum would serve nobody well. She crouched down. "Perhaps you could tell me where he is."

Millie shook her head. "No, I have to take you. He said so."

"Millie, I said it's time to go. Now say goodbye to Jasmine and help me put the tools in the shed."

Millie folded her arms and pouted. "Don't want to."

Jaz itched to dash off and find Rick, but without Millie she'd no idea where to look. "Please, Ted. A couple of minutes, while you put the tools away. We'll be quick."

Ted rubbed his chin and looked at his watch. "I don't know what you two are up to, but you'd better be quick. I'll do a bit of leaf blowing over yonder. That'll give you ten minutes. No more."

"Thanks, Ted." Jaz thrust the lettuce and blackcurrants into his arms, grabbed Millie's hand and trotted beside her down the path.

As they approached the fairy house, Millie stopped. "Oh, no."

"What's wrong?"

"The door's open." Millie ran across to the house and lifted the roof. "Wic! Wic where are you?"

Her eyes welled with tears. "Jasmy, he's gone. Wic's gone. He said he'd wait."

Jaz's heart nose-dived. She dropped to her knees and peered into the house, lifted one of the four-poster beds and looked underneath. "Are you sure he was here?"

Millie gave her a withering look. "He's a naughty pixie. He's wun away."

"Rick, can you hear me?" Jaz called, and listened for a reply.

"My pixie's gone." Millie's bottom lip trembled. "I want him back."

Jaz squeezed her hand. "Let's see if we can find him. He can't have gone far." She crawled across the grass, lifting leaves that skimmed the ground and disturbing insects. Millie closed the roof and the front door and then followed Jaz, calling his name with her small, high-pitched voice.

And then Jaz heard a faint sound, not insects, not birds. A tiny voice calling her name. She turned in its direction and scoured the ground, until she spotted him, only metres away. A little man in tattered wet clothes jumped up and down waving. Relief swept through her, her stomach bubbled with excitement, tears of joy sprang to her eyes. As soon as they found Whisper and Balmanza, Rick would be restored to full height.

"Look, he's there, Millie." She pointed. "Be careful. Don't stand on him."

Millie beamed. "See, I told you. He's my pixie. If you're good you can hold him."

Jaz stood up and began walking slowly towards him, not wanting to make the ground vibrate too much or scare him with her enormous size. Millie tiptoed at her side. Jaz couldn't wait to tell him her story and hear his. Thank God he was all right.

Rick jogged towards them, his little legs covering hardly any distance. The look on his face spoke volumes, his smile couldn't have been wider or his eyes brighter.

In a blur of blue-black feathers a bird plunged down, talons spread. It swooped past Jaz, bare inches from her face. Raising her free hand to protect herself, she shrieked, recoiled and dragged Millie with her. When Jaz recovered and looked down at the ground Rick had vanished.

Chapter Twenty-Four

Rick hardly had time to register what was happening. One second running towards Jaz and Millie, bursting with joy at being rescued, the next clutched in the talons of a bird and whisked into the air.

"Put me down, let me go," he yelled at the bird as it flapped its wings and rose higher. Far below he could see Jaz running through the garden chasing after them.

So close. He'd almost been rescued. He'd expected Millie to bring a tiny Jaz to him, and could hardly believe his eyes when she'd been her normal size. Had the magic worn off of its own accord, or had she found an antidote? Who cared as long as it worked for him too?

He wriggled around and beat on the bird's talons with his fists. The bird squawked and held him tighter. He'd thought the wasp had been a formidable foe, but at least then he'd had the sword, now he had nothing. Being this low on the food chain was no fun at all.

He managed to manoeuvre into a position where his head rested on a talon. He eyed up the bird's scaly leg, opened his mouth wide and sank his teeth into the flesh, clamping his jaw as tightly as possible. Warm, metallic tasting blood gushed into his mouth and down his throat. He gagged. The bird squawked and loosened its grip.

Rick opened his mouth, spat out the blood, and wiped his mouth with the back of his hand. He dismissed thoughts of diseases that could cross from birds to humans. Once again he attacked the leg, sinking his teeth in deep and tearing off a strip of raw flesh. Bile rose in his throat, its bitter taste mingling with that of the blood. Survival of the fittest. He had no choice but to carry on if he didn't want to become bird food.

The bird dropped towards the ground, veering across the meadow behind Jaz's garden. He spotted her racing towards the stile. At first, he thought she was waving at him, then he saw her throwing stones at the bird. The next stone missed the bird by a matter of inches. Rick bit again, and spat another chunk of bird leg away. The leg dripped blood, the bird cried out and as Rick hit the shredded limb with his fist, a stone caught its wing. The bird eddied, swooping downwards and releasing him, before beating its wings and soaring away.

"Oh, shit!" Rick hadn't considered what would happen when the bird dropped him. He tumbled downwards, flapping his arms, wishing he could fly or at least had a parachute. He heard Jaz screaming his name, saw her running across the meadow, but the bird hadn't released him above the meadow. The river flowed below him, and he plunged towards the watery landing with no means of escape.

He held his breath as his body crashed through the surface and the water covered his head sucking him deep into its murky depths. He kicked and kicked, and headed towards the light, his burning lungs threatening to burst. Coughing and spluttering he burst into the air and flicked his hair out of his eyes, treading water, trying to get his bearings.

"Just my bloody luck!" He'd managed to land slap bang in the middle of the river. Not a strong swimmer, he doubted if he could reach either bank. He had no choice, though. Swim for the shore or be carried away on the current. He faced the meadow and began splashing towards it, swearing that if he made it back in one piece he'd have some lessons and learn to swim properly.

Chapter Twenty-Five

"Nooooo!" Jaz screamed. Her stomach free-fell in sympathy when she saw Rick rocket towards the river and barely make a splash as he broke the surface and disappeared. Puffing and panting, she trampled cornflowers and poppies underfoot running as fast as she could towards the riverbank focussing on the spot where Rick had immersed. When, coughing and spluttering, arms flailing, he bobbed up like a cork, she cheered. The lazy river meandered slowly. With any luck the current wouldn't carry him too far downstream. "Swim, Rick, swim!"

"Jasmy, where's Wic? Where is he?"

Jaz stopped running and turned around. She'd left Millie to fend for herself the minute the bird had snatched Rick into the air. Somehow the little girl had negotiated the stile and now, red-faced and sweaty, she ran through the long grass along a rabbit track.

"He's in the water."

Behind Millie, at the far side of the meadow, Jaz spotted Annabel practically vaulting over the stile, more agile than Jaz would have given her credit for. Jaz scowled. Why hadn't she left? She didn't want to explain Rick's diminutive size to the art dealer, but it looked like she'd have no option. Maybe Millie could persuade her that he really was Wic the pixie. Annabel's spike heels should have slowed her down, but watching the way she traversed the uneven terrain at the edge of the meadow, they could have been hiking boots.

Lifting her hair, damp with sweat, off the back of her neck Jaz returned her attention to the river, where Rick treaded water. He hadn't started swimming. The expanse of water would look like the English Channel to someone his size, but he was wasting energy. "Swim," she screeched.

Millie reached the riverbank. Automatically, Jaz grabbed her shoulders and made her take a couple of steps away from the edge. "Not too close. We don't want you falling in, too."

"Swim, Wic. Swim to me." Millie jumped up and down, then she began to giggle. "He looks funny."

Dismayed, Jaz watched Rick's hopeless doggy paddle. He didn't look funny; he looked pathetic. Despite all his obvious effort, he was making little progress.

In the distance, thunder rumbled. She looked at the sky. Thick, black clouds banded together, blocking the sun, stealing the blue. In spite of the heat, she shivered, and rubbed at the scar tissue on her shoulder. A storm. Coming for her. She glanced from the river to the house. She'd be safe in the house. Then she remembered the crails. Maybe not.

"Miaow." Whisper nudged her ankle. She scooped him up.

"Where have you been?" She stroked his head and pulled a bur from his fur. "Rick's in the water. We have to save him."

Whisper hopped from her arms, sat down, licked a paw and washed his ear. His eyes narrowed as he cocked his head. "Miaooow."

She took that to mean _Don't look at me_. Typical cat. Whisper hated water. She'd bathed him once and ended up covered in blood from his slashing claws.

"Jasmy, Wic's a vewy bad swimmer."

"I can see that." She chewed on the skin around her fingernail.

"You need to save him."

"I can't." Jaz trembled, her heart raced, her breath short. No way could she go in that river, not after last time. She stepped backwards and squealed when she bumped into Annabel. She pivoted around. "Shit! You frightened the life out of me. I didn't realise you'd covered the distance so quickly."

Unperturbed, Annabel asked, "What are we looking at?".

"Wic." Millie pointed. "He's my pixie. He's not a good swimmer."

Annabel's eyes scanned the surface, until they locked on Rick. "Possibly the worst swimmer I've ever seen. He'll drown for sure."

Surprised by Annabel's lack of amazement at Rick's tiny stature, Jaz glanced at her, but before she had chance to comment, Millie spoke. "Jasmy's going to save him."

Thunder clapped. Closer this time. Jaz clutched her throat, trying to stop hyperventilating. "I'm not. I can't."

Rick had covered a quarter of the distance to the shore, but the signs of exhaustion became evident. Each stroke slower, shorter than the last. Annabel was right; he couldn't possibly make the riverbank. He'd drown.

"Gwandad says you swim good. You can wescue him."

"Not any more. I don't swim in the river."

A dragonfly skimmed the water surface, barely missing Rick. He raised his arms in defence then foundered. The river swallowed him.

Millie screamed. Tears erupted from her eyes. She yanked on Jaz's hand. "Jasmy. Get him. Save my pixie. Save him."

Jaz scoured the surface. Thought she'd spotted him then realised it was a twig. Then his head burst out of the water, arms waving uselessly above his head. He went under a second time. Jaz's heart lurched, but her feet had taken root. She willed herself forward, but fear immobolised her. Rick emerged again, this time legs and arms splashing with renewed effort, but fatigue could only be minutes away. If he went under again it might be for the last time.

Sweat trickled down Jaz's spine, her nerves quivered.

Frantic, jumping up and down and clutching her curls, Millie cried and implored. "Save him. Save Wic. You have to, Jasmy. You have to. You the gwown-up. I'm too little."

"Looks like it's down to you," said Annabel, picking a bit of dirt from under her nail and flicking it away.

How could she look so nonchalant? Rick's life was in danger.

"I can't go in the river, Annabel. You go."

Annabel's lip curled. "No way. He's nothing to me. I don't care if he lives or dies."

Jaz's eyes widened, her jaw dropped. Thunder cracked, the claps closer together, the storm was moving in. Moving in for the kill. She looked around for help, but there was nobody. Rick's doggy paddle had slowed even more and he struggled to keep his head above water.

"Go, Jasmy, go." Millie pushed Jaz towards the edge. Jaz stumbled forward.

"I can't do it."

"You have to." Millie pushed again, amazing Jaz with the force her tiny body exerted. "Go."

"Whisper, get Balmanza." The genie could help. Where the hell was he? Never around when she needed him. Whisper got to his feet, stretched and trotted away. "Faster, Whisper. Run for God's sake."

The first drops of rain fell, big and heavy, exploding like supernovas, churning the water. A massive drop burst on Rick's head and he spluttered and splashed. Jaz realised she'd no option. If she didn't go, he'd die and she'd be responsible. She kicked off her shoes, and sucking in a deep breath ran to the edge, jumped in without hesitating, gasping as the water cooled her hot clammy skin. Eyes fixed on Rick's position she struck out with a long smooth stroke never veering. The thunder roared in her ears. A short distance from him, in order to cause fewer ripples, she slowed her pace. Then before her eyes he sank.

Her heart raced. "No. You can't have him," she screamed at the river. Filling her lungs with air, she duck dived and searched the churning water, her chest threatening to burst before she spotted him. She snatched him and made for the surface.

Treading water, she caught her breath. On her palm, Rick lay inert, eyes rolled back so she could see the whites, his chest unmoving. She had to get him back to shore and pump his lungs. She should have come sooner, shouldn't have hesitated. She choked back tears. No time to cry. She lay his prone body on top of her head, cushioned by her hair, and then keeping as level as possible, headed back to the riverbank, where Millie was clapping her hands and jumping for joy.

Chapter Twenty-Six

"Millie, take Rick." Jaz took his inert body and passed him to the little girl. She hoisted herself onto the riverbank, almost falling back into the water when a massive thunderclap roared.

Millie prodded Rick, then shook him. "Jasmy, he's not moving."

"Be careful with him!" Jaz dropped to her knees, grabbed Millie's hand and held her palm flat. The colour had drained from Rick's face, his chest didn't move. *Don't be dead, don't be dead.* Terrified of applying too much pressure and crushing his ribs, she used her ring finger and began compressions.

She bent her face to his wondering if she could safely administer the kiss of life. His head, impossibly small, no bigger than a raspberry, had begun to turn blue. She had no choice. Whisper hadn't returned with Balmanza, and she'd no idea if the genie could bring someone back from the dead. She blew the tiniest breath into Rick's mouth, felt his chest rise then fall.

Alternating between compressions and inflating his lungs, her world shrunk. She couldn't let him die. She'd dragged him into this mess. She'd known there was something weird about the house since Whisper vanished into the wall. Still, without knowing with what she was dealing, she'd invited him into the house, and made no attempt to explain any of the strange phenomena.

A tear escaped the net of her eyelashes and splattered his face. Before she could wipe it away, Rick spluttered and coughed water onto Millie's palm.

"Yucky! He's spitting on me."

Relief swamped Jaz, making her knees weak. She slumped onto her heels. "It's good it means he's okay. He's alive."

Rick pushed himself to a sitting position.

"Good. You're better." Millie kissed him, transferred him to her free hand and wiped her wet palm on her clothes.

Annabel leant over Jaz, proffering a hip flask. "Brandy, good for shock."

"Thanks." Jaz poured a capful and handed it to Rick. With both hands he held the cap in front of his chest. It looked like a bucket of brandy, too big to tip to his mouth. Catlike he lapped at the liquid, and colour returned to his cheeks.

"Okay. That's enough medicinal brandy for you," Jaz laughed, taking the cap from him. She downed the measure in a gulp. Blinked at the sharp heat as it rolled over her tongue and down her throat. She handed the cap to Annabel, and wondered at her composure. Annabel hadn't shown a flicker of surprise at Rick's stature. Jaz's eyes narrowed. Any normal person would have been intrigued by the little man, but Annabel hadn't batted an eyelid.

"Will someone tell me what's going on?" asked Rick. "Why am I so small?"

Jaz looked at the gathering black clouds and crossing her arms hugged herself, suddenly aware of her wet clothes. "I'll explain when we get back to the house. There's a storm about to break."

"Whisper's coming. Ooh, he's on fire." Millie pointed across the meadow to where Whisper bounded along a rabbit track. He did indeed look to be on fire, he ran so fast he looked like he was trying to outrun the orange flames that flickered along his length.

"He's not on fire, that's Balmanza," said Jaz. "Everything will be all right now. Balmanza will return you to normal size, Rick."

"Who?"

Jaz pointed. "Balmanza. Whisper's genie."

"As in rub the magic lamp?"

"Sort of."

"Tell me I'm dreaming. This is crazy."

"Sorry. It's real. Crazy but real. I don't really understand it either. What about you Annabel? You seem pretty unfazed."

Annabel peered down her nose at Rick, her lip curled. "Nothing I haven't seen before. A lot of fuss over very little if you ask me."

Jaz's jaw worked but she couldn't find words to express herself. Annabel's rudeness was on a completely different scale to Millie's.

"Isn't that your gardener?" asked Annabel.

Jaz turned to see Ted clambering over the stile, encumbered by a leaf blower. "Millie! Stay away from those flames."

"Gwandad. We found my pixie. Jaz wescued him." Millie waved Rick at Ted.

"Woah, Millie. You're going to make me puke." Rick clung to her finger.

Whisper stopped in front of Jaz. Balmanza twisted into a ball and hovered by Whisper's tail. She bent to stroke her pet. "Well done. Now, I need you to ask Balmanza to return Rick to normal size."

A flash of lightning split the sky. Jaz ducked.

Annabel moved towards Whisper, her eyes wide and shining. "So, Balmanza, finally we meet again."

Balmanza stretched towards Annabel and then recoiled. He spun around, his colours blazing brighter than ever. "Nareel. How did you find me?"

Annabel sneered. "I've been searching for you for centuries, and then I recognised *my* bottle in Teri's painting. I knew she had it somewhere."

"My bottle?" asked Jaz.

"It was never yours!" Annabel spat. "It was stolen from me. Now I've come to reclaim my property."

"I already told you, the bottle broke."

"Not the bottle, the genie."

"Balmanza, who is she? What's going on?"

Balmanza undulated, changing from red to orange and back again. "Her name is Nareel, she is a great sorceress. She has many powers of her own, but some things I can accomplish that even she cannot. She owned me from the beginning of time, but a thief stole the bottle and she lost track of me for millennia."

Annabel huffed. "An interesting interlude for you, I'm sure."

A finger of lightning arced above the river, as the storm moved closer.

"Whisper is my master." Balmanza bellowed, shaking the ground.

"But now I'm reclaiming you. We have work to do."

"You can't have him, he belongs to Whisper." Jaz pointed to Whisper, who crouched, focussed on Annabel, his body twitching. "He's his master."

"Not for much longer," laughed Annabel.

Whisper leapt at her his teeth and claws flashing. Annabel dodged. He twisted and prepared for another attack. She pulled a triangular piece of glistening blue-edged steel from her pocket and with a flick of her wrist flung it at Whisper. Mid leap, the blade split his skull, embedded between his ears. Jaz screamed. Whisper's eyes rolled and he fell, his feet touched the ground, but his legs gave way, and he collapsed onto the grass, blood seeping into the dry earth.

Chapter Twenty-Seven

"You bitch!" Jaz flung herself at Annabel, fists ready to pummel her face to a pulp. In the blink of an eye, Annabel had turned from a potential friend into Jaz's nemesis.

Annabel's lip curled, she made a dismissive gesture with her hand as though shooing a fly. A mighty force slammed into Jaz's chest knocking her off her feet and tumbling her onto her rear. Winded, she rubbed her elbow where it had struck a stone, her fingers came away bloody.

Millie screamed and ran towards Whisper, but Ted grabbed her, dropped to his knees, turned her crumpled face into his chest and hugged her tight. The little girl broke into loud, body shaking sobs, clinging to Ted's shirtsleeve with one hand and squeezing Rick with the other. Rick squeaked his displeasure.

Annabel uncapped the silver hip flask, upended it, pouring the amber liquid onto the grass. "Now the cat's dead, Balmanza, you're mine again. This time smashed glass won't free you. You'll not be able to escape from this container. You'll be at my beck and call once more."

Balmanza hovered by Whisper. Moments ago his colours had burnt bright, but when the last drops of life drained from Whisper, the genie darkened and dimmed.

"Come. Now. It's almost time for us to leave." As the thunder roared and a bolt of lightning raced to earth, Annabel waved the flask and said some words Jaz couldn't grasp in a language she'd not heard before. Balmanza's essence began to twist and turn, slithering towards the flask in a long thin streak of dull colour. He moved so slowly Jaz could tell he was resisting with all his might, but even with his amazing power he was helpless against Annabel's will.

"Aisha, Aisha." Against the incessant rumbling of thunder, eerie voices pierced the air, making the little hairs on the back of Jaz's neck stand on end. Crails. Her head turned in their direction, her gaze settling on the house where she spotted the dark shapes of several emerging from the chimney, like the blackest of black puffs of smoke. Once in the open air their shapes stretched out, and took on the familiar leaf shape, like giant manta rays gliding silently through the sky. A wave of horror engulfed her body, and she grasped her throat. They were coming for her.

They swept across the inky darkness and circled the group. The last of Balmanza slithered into the flask. A smile of satisfaction spread across Annabel's face as she screwed the cap into place. In triumph she held the flask aloft and gloated. Joining her celebration the crails fluttered in appreciation, the draft they created whipping the grass from side to side.

Distraught, Jaz didn't know what to do. Her enemies showed no signs of leaving. What more did they want? Looking from one to the other of her friends her throat swelled so much it threatened her breathing. She swallowed, trying to stifle her rising emotions. Her beloved Whisper: murdered. Rick: miniscule. Millie: distraught. Ted: stunned. Balmanza: imprisoned. People she loved and cared about all hurt by Annabel and the crails.

She had to do something to save her friends, but she was one person against a band of timeless beings with magical powers. She knew when she was beaten. Losing Whisper and Balmanza was too painful. She couldn't resurrect Whisper, and though Balmanza drove her nuts, she'd developed a fondness for the genie and liked having him around. He and Whisper were a great double act. Or they had been.

After mere days of freedom with Whisper, Balmanza had once more become Nareel's slave and been incarcerated in a bottle. Jaz knew how that felt. She needed to find a way to release Balmanza from the sorceress's clutches. They'd been locked in their battle since the beginning of time. She couldn't contend. Her heart contracted. Whisper. Balmanza. She'd be grieving their loss for many a day. She couldn't pay an even bigger price by risking further retribution on Rick and Millie and Ted.

From her place on the ground, she looked up at Annabel. "You've got what you wanted. Now piss off and leave us alone."

"The key." Annabel held out her open palm. "Give me the key."

It wasn't over.

Jaz shook her head. "I don't know what you're talking about."

"The key to the box. I know you have it."

"I don't. I've never seen it."

"Aishaaaaaaa." A crail moved towards her.

She wouldn't go down without a fight. Wouldn't be shrunk again. She'd die first. Impelled by fury, she jumped to her feet. Lightning flashed all around, distorting Annabel's face into a twisted leer. Jaz didn't know which scared her most: the lightning or Annabel and the crails. "I haven't got your bloody key. Go. Leave us alone."

Millie wriggled from Ted's grip, grabbed Jaz's hand and tugged on it. "Jasmy."

"Not now, Millie." She pushed Millie behind her, shielding the child's body with her own.

"Please, Jasmy. I want to whisper you something."

"Later."

"Now."

Millie dodged in front of Jaz and stomped on her foot. Jaz blinked, howled and bent to rub her toes.

"You need to teach this child some manners, Ted."

Ted rubbed his forehead. "Soon as we're out of this mess. What's this key stuff?"

"Some Pandora thing. It's the key that let all the good stuff into the world. If they get it back they can lock it all up again and the world will be left with only the crap."

"Don't you dare give her the key," Ted and Rick spoke together.

Jaz rolled her eyes, flicking her hands out in exasperation. "How many times do I have to say it? I haven't got the damn key!"

Millie pulled Jaz's wrist until Jaz bent down. The child put her arm around Jaz's neck and whispered in her ear. "It's in your pocket."

"What is?"

"The key."

Laughing, Jaz dislodged Millie's hand and stood up. She put her hand in her pocket, pulled out the letter opener and her key ring. "These are for the house."

"I knew you had it," screeched Annabel, dashing across the few metres of grass that separated them.

"They're house keys," said Jaz, waving the two keys on their chain.

"The other one, you fool."

Annabel reached out to snatch the letter opener from Jaz. Jaz feinted managing to dodge Annabel's grasp.

"It's a letter opener," said Jaz.

"It's the key. It belongs to me."

"No chance." She stuffed it back into her pocket.

Another bolt of lightning flashed, ripping the belly of the sky, releasing a torrent of rain. Plump drops fell, their torrential force drenching Jaz in a second, the wind rose whipping her wet hair across her face, stinging her cheeks. Jaz glanced at the grumbling sky. Strident thunderclaps roared one over the other, in a constant rolling dissonance. Lightning chased, so close, too close. Jaz shuddered. Her scar tissue tingled. She had to get away. Away from the lightning. Before it got her.

Jaz ran.

"Get her!" Annabel commanded the crails.

Jaz felt the crails beating the sky, saw their shadows dance across her path. If she tried to escape she couldn't outrun them. If they killed her they'd get the key anyway. She'd no option. This way she might live.

She spun around, ready to surrender.

"Stop!" she yelled at the crails. Her arms flung forward, fingers splayed. Rain hammered on her body like a thousand needles. A fork of lightning tore towards her, then struck. It entered her chest, its searing vitality shot across her body, down her arms, and out of her fingertips slamming into one of the crails. The creature screeched and fell to the ground. Amazed that the lightning hadn't cremated her, and delighted to have killed a crail, she thrust her fingers forward again, aiming at her prey. The tables had turned. Time and time again, lightning shot from her fingers, destroying one crail after another as they fought to overpower her.

As the last one crumpled and plummeted at her feet, a sense of empowerment surged through Jaz. Intuitively she knew how to direct and control the lightning coursing through her body. Her nerves tingled from head to toe. She'd never felt more alive. With this new ability she could do anything. Nothing could stop her now.

"Damn you!" Annabel's face contorted, her eyes blazed. She flicked her free hand towards Jaz.

"I'm not falling for that trick twice." Before the force could knock her to the ground again, Jaz pointed her index finger and lightning shot towards Annabel's hand, impacting on the invisible force and turning it into a field of sparking fireflies that dispersed into the darkness.

"You've seen nothing yet," Annabel hissed.

"Bring it on, bitch. Nobody kills my cat and gets away with it."

"You tell her, Jaz," shouted Rick. "Show her what you're made of."

Annabel made a humming sound, then opened her mouth wide, a blur of movement poured from her lips as a swarm of angry wasps flew out, homing in on Jaz. Jaz fired bolt after bolt of lightning, but managed to only take out a couple at a time. The first sting set her cheek on fire. She beat the wasp away as another made a successful hit on her elbow. She screamed in fury trying to bat them away.

A motor roared into life. "I'll deal with this." Ted ran towards her holding the leaf blower in front of him like a weapon.

"Will it blow them away?" asked Rick.

"I've set it to suck." Ted swung the leaf blower towards Jaz, the fabric of her clothes pulled towards it as he played the nozzle over her body sucking the swarming creatures into the bag. "Keep fighting, lass. Don't give in."

Jaz rubbed her swelling cheek, her gaze locked on Annabel who dabbed the corners of her mouth with a red taloned finger. "I don't know what to do next, Ted."

"You'll come up with something." Ted patted her on the back, as the last wasp disappeared up the nozzle. "Go to it."

Jaz held up her hands, ready to loose more lightning, but gasped as tears burst from Annabel's eyes. "My God, she's crying. Maybe it's over."

"I don't think so," said Ted, inching way.

The tears didn't fall, didn't slide down her cheeks, and drip from her chin. They exploded outwards, shiny and bright, turning into hailstones the size of golf balls. Millie screamed. Ted dropped the leaf blower, hurtled over and snatched her into his arms. Reaching a tree, he plonked her against the trunk using his body to protect her from the cascading hail. Millie wailed.

Jaz set off following Ted, but realised she was drawing the hailstones towards her friends. She changed direction, looking for cover, but the meadow offered little but grass and wild flowers. Hail slammed into her, forcing the breath from her body. The stones formed a deepening carpet at her feet, the ice biting into her bare flesh, at once stinging her and making her shiver. Her breath froze in front of her face. She hugged herself, but unable to resist the cold, her legs gave way and she fell down, her vision blurring as her strength ebbed.

She pointed her shaking fingers at Annabel, but could no longer channel the lightning. The cold impaired her ability to control it, to control anything. As her power slipped away, Annabel's high-pitched laugh carried through the darkness. She tossed her hip flask from hand to hand. "Give me the key, and the pain will stop."

Jaz wished she could free Balmanza. The genie might be a bit too cocky for her liking, but he did have his uses. On the other hand he'd been no match for Annabel. He had to obey her commands whether he wanted to or not. Jaz had no one to rely on, no one to help her. Rick was too small to be of use, and Ted had to protect Millie. If she gave Annabel the key they'd survive.

"You mean this key?" Her teeth chattered, as she pulled the jewelled letter opener from her pocket. She glanced at the shiny metal. Through her frost-encased eyelashes the stones sparkled. What she'd assumed was brass and glass, she now suspected was gold and jewels. If she handed it over, the world would be plunged into an abyss of cruelty, pestilence and war. Nothing good would ever happen again. She clasped it to her heart. "No chance. I'll never relinquish it."

"It's a matter of time. You can give it me now and live or I can wait until you die. It shouldn't be long now, you're already turning blue."

Jaz hardly noticed when the hail stopped bombarding her. Annabel glided across the ice until she towered over her. She prodded Jaz's hip with the pointed toe of her shoe.

"You'll freeze for all eternity, Aisha, and the key will be mine."

In Jaz's curled fingers, the key throbbed, heat emanated from the stones and permeated her hands and her chest, travelling through her veins, warming her blood and supplying her with strength. She took a deep breath and energy saturated her soul.

She kicked Annabel's foot away and jumped up. "Don't dare touch me again."

Annabel took a step back, her eyes wide.

Jaz held the top of the key tightly. "You want this key?"

"You know I do. We could share the power."

"Here you are then." Using all her strength Jaz stabbed the pointed end of the key into the back of Annabel's hand.

Annabel screeched and dropped the hip flask. Blood as black as tar dripped from the wound. Her face contorted. She clutched at her throat, gasping for breath. Her body writhed and twisted and she collapsed on the ground, her legs spasming.

Jaz snatched up the hip flask and unscrewed the cap. "Balmanza, come out. It's Jaz."

A beam of light shone from the neck of the flask and then the genie slithered out. Once free, he soared around the meadow, his colours glowing. For a few seconds, he hovered over Whisper's corpse. His colours dimmed and pulsed before brightening and he flew off again.

"Stop messing about and come back here," shouted Jaz. "We need help."

Balmanza stopped dead, and then homed in on Jaz. "Mistress, thank you for releasing me. What is your desire?"

"Mistress? Does that mean you're my genie now?"

"Yes, Mistress."

Yes! She had her own genie. She jumped up and high fived the air. "Excellent. I want rid of Annabel."

"Who?"

"Her." Jaz pointed. "What did you call her? Nareel?"

"It doesn't look like you need any help from me. What did you do?"

"I stabbed her with the key."

Ted, carrying Millie, who still held onto Rick, joined them. "She looks in a bad way. Her skins withering."

"She's not dead yet, though," said Rick. "You were brilliant, Jaz. I thought you were done for at one point."

"Me too," she said. She examined the key. "I can't believe stabbing her did this."

"It's the power of the key." Balmanza glowed bright orange. "You stabbed her full of goodness. For Nareel, you couldn't have found a worse poison. There's no antidote. She'll die soon."

Millie squirmed in Ted's arms and he put her down. "Don't go near her."

"While we're waiting, any chance you could have me returned to normal size?" asked Rick.

"Then you won't be my pixie." Millie put him into her pocket. "You have to stay small."

"Millie, let me out. We can still be friends."

She stamped her foot. "But I've got fwiends. I'd wather have a pixie."

"Millie!"

Millie jumped up and down and laughed. "Look, it's Whisper."

"Miaow, miaow." Whisper trotted across the ice. Jaz ran to him, skidded to a halt and scooped him into her arms, smothering him in kisses. "Oh Whisper, you're alive. You're alive."

Balmanza coughed.

"Did you do this?" asked Jaz.

The genie flashed through his colour range. "I helped. He's got six lives left."

Jaz bent to Millie. "Would you like to hold Whisper?"

The little girl held her arms out.

"I'll swap you for Rick."

"But he's my pixie."

"I know, but he needs to be made man size. I bet once he's big he'll give you piggy back rides."

"I will, I will," Rick's muffled voice came for inside Millie's pocket.

"Okay, and you have to push me really high on the swing."

"Deal."

Chapter Twenty-Eight

They spent the night together in Jaz's lounge, reliving their stories, bonded by their experience. In the early hours the storm burnt out. First Millie, then Ted and finally Rick fell asleep, but Jaz couldn't switch off. She crept out of the room and went outside and sat on a wet garden chair with Whisper on her lap. Near by, pale yellow the size of a mango, Balmanza hovered. Together they watched the dawn break. The world smelled fresh and clean.

At the sound of footsteps she turned. Rick, back to normal size, handed her a mug of tea. He sat down beside her and rubbed his stubbly chin. "I must have dozed off. For a second, I thought the crails had taken you."

"I couldn't sleep." She sipped the tea, hot and sweet. "Ted was snoring so loud."

"He and Millie are still in the land of nod. He should have taken her home."

"He wants her to see the end so that she knows it's over and that we were more powerful than the monsters. He's hoping she'll be less traumatised in the long run. Besides, she wanted to make sure you made good on your promise."

"She wore me out. Piggy back rides were a dumb idea."

"Stop complaining. At least you're not a pixie for life."

"True." He drained his tea. "What will you do about your mother's paintings now?"

"Look for a new dealer. It shouldn't be hard to find one. I Googled her. She was a much bigger deal than I ever realised. At least I'll be able to keep this place."

Rick's eyes widened. "You're going to stay here after all that's happened?"

"Why not? I've got Whisper and Balmanza and the key. Not to mention the lightning. Practically invincible," she laughed.

Rick stood and stretched. "The concrete mixer will be here soon."

"So early?"

"Tony owed me a couple of favours."

"I'll be in in a second."

Jaz slid Whisper to the ground and walked through the garden. He walked beside her, miaowing occasionally.

"Can you believe what happened?" She flicked her fingers out. Nothing happened. "I wonder if I'll be able to channel lightning next time there's a storm? Maybe it's a one off."

She leant on the stile and looked at the meadow. The long grass rippled, dew drops glistened in the weak sunshine. Tranquil. No sign of the battle that had raged only hours ago.

In the distance an engine rumbled. "Come on. That must be the cement mixer."

When she entered the house, Ted and Millie were awake. "Jasmy, come and look."

"Millie, one thing I don't understand," said Jaz. "How did you know the letter opener was a key?"

"Tewi give it me. She said Nanalu made the little one the same for the faiwy house. It opens it." She rooted in her pocket and pulled out a sticky toffee wrapper, a tiny plastic puppy, and a miniature replica of the key. "See. It's the same."

Jaz took the little key and held it to the light. She pulled out the full size one. "You're right. It's a perfect copy. Just smaller."

She gave it back to Millie, wondering if it too was infused with goodness. "Keep it safe."

Millie stuffed it back in her pocket with the toy puppy. "Are you ready?" asked Rick.

Jaz dipped her chin. Balmanza flickered. Ted picked up the leaf blower. He'd sucked up the remains of the crails once Annabel had died. At Jaz's command, Balmanza had shrunk Annabel's wasted corpse until she could be squeezed into the hip flask, Jaz had sealed the cap with superglue and then kept the flask in her pocket. She couldn't fully trust that she'd won. That Annabel was gone for good.

Jaz took a deep breath and opened the library door, expecting to gag on the putrid air, but the smell had diminished, leaving only a faint stale odour behind. She walked into the room. Rick pushed past her and opened the window and the hose from the churning cement mixer fed through. He hefted the hose onto his shoulder, pulled it across the room, through the broken wall and rested the end over the open well.

"We're ready to roll," he said.

Whisper skipped over the rubble, and the others followed. They stood around the edge, looking into the cavity, the green light had dimmed and the slime had receded. Ted tossed the leaf blower into the pit. "Good riddance."

It careened off the side but stayed intact as it clattered to a halt at the bottom.

The hip flask weighed heavy in Jaz's hand as she tugged it from her pocket. In death, shrunk and encased in the flask, Annabel emitted a sense of evil. Jaz shuddered and let the flask slide from her fingers into the depths.

"Okay, Tony. We're on," called Rick. The pump spluttered into action and then thick grey concrete poured from the hose, splattering the sides of the well and burying Annabel and the crails forever.

"Now it's over," said Jaz.

"Miaow," said Whisper.

Other Books by Jessica Hemingway

Consumed

In drought-ridden New Zealand, Detective Ashley North finds herself in a race against time when she investigates an unexplained death in a small rural town. The corpse's internal organs have been ravaged and a new virus is suspected. To avoid panic, the decision is made to keep the news of the virus from the public, but investigative journalist Mike Donovan has other ideas.

Ashley's workload increases and things go from bad to worse as more victims are discovered. To find the source before New Zealand's population is decimated she and Donovan must join forces.

The Beadmaker

Unable to cope with her abusive family any longer, sixteen year old Georgie runs away. Two decades later, her grandfather is dying. Now a successful artist living in Hawaii, Gina Glass returns to the North of England for the first time. Back in the family home she must face her demons and reassess her relationships with her grieving relatives. Whilst dealing with her past she meets Dariel Varik, a young Parisian art dealer who offers her a foothold into the future.

Will Dariel open the door to the coveted European art market for her or does he have a different agenda? As Gina tries to heal the rifts in her family, secrets are exposed, and only the truth will save her.

Coming in 2014

Spirit Of Obsession

Stella McBride doesn't believe in ghosts or psychic phenomena. About to be married she has no time for such nonsense. But when light bulbs start blowing, mirrors fall off walls and radios turn on by themselves she begins to wonder if she might be wrong. When ex-lover Rhett Harrison sends her a message via a psychic her world is turned upside down.

Obsessed by the messages and solving the puzzle they contain Stella is determined to discover what happened to Rhett. She becomes embroiled in mystery and is drawn into a dark world where she must choose between following Rhett or life.

Words to Write

When budding author, Carla Quinn, is challenged to write a book in a month she thinks she's up to the task, but she hasn't bargained for everything that will prevent her reaching her deadline. A born procrastinator, Carla makes a slow start but as her story gathers speed her distractions mount. Between the demands of her family, friends, pets, job at a rest home, and training for a marathon, diversions abound.

And then there's a personal problem to be solved that could spell the end of her marriage.

Will Carla reach her goal or will the trials of life prove too much to handle?

 facebook.com/ jessicahemingwayauthor

 twitter.com/jessicahemingwy

www.ingramcontent.com/pod-product-compliance
Lightning Source LLC
Chambersburg PA
CBHW021105130626
46554CB00002B/537